# BRAIN GAIN

## A HIGH-STAKES TECHNOTHRILLER

## GERALD M. KILBY

OUTER PLANET
MEDIA

Published by GMK, 2024

Version 1.0

For notifications on upcoming books, and access to my FREE starter library,
please join my Readers Group at geraldmkilby.com.

# ALSO BY GERALD M. KILBY

# CHAPTER 1
# PLEASE REMAIN CALM

Dawn Harrison awoke to blinding white light—harsh and clinical. As her eyes slowly adjusted to the intensity of the brightness, her brain figured out that she was lying on her back in a hospital bed. A crisp, white sheet covered her body, her upper torso was elevated, and her head rested on a soft foam pillow. She glanced down to see both arms exposed. From one, a cannula had been inserted just above her right wrist, with a plastic tube snaking its way up to an IV drip. From the other, wires trailed from various probes to a monitor at the side of her bed that traced her life in waves and datagrams.

*What's happened to me?* A panicked thought rose in her mind. *Where am I?*

She searched her brain for an answer but it came back blank—nothing. She had no memory of what had happened to her or why she'd ended up lying in a hospital bed. She tried again, desperate to seek out some clue, but there was nothing tangible, nothing concrete, nothing to grab hold of. Except... somewhere in the deepest recesses of her mind was the vaguest hint of a car crash, a distant memory of some horrific trauma still imprinted on her brain. Yet, it was nothing more than a feeling. There was no visual imagery she could manifest to add weight to this incident. Still, it seemed to Dawn to be the most rational explanation, and with it came visions of mangled metal strewn across a roadway, of a shattered, hissing machine buried deep into a highway barrier. These visions prompted a harrowing thought in her mind, one of serious, life-changing injury.

She glanced down at her right arm, then sent a tentative signal to her hand; it responded by clenching into a weak fist— as did her left hand. She breathed an internal sigh of relief. Then, she sent another probe down to her feet and saw the humps in the sheet move left and right. She relaxed a little more; she was still whole and functioning.

Yet, here she was, so something must have happened to her. Perhaps she had sustained a head injury, possibly a concussion? *Yes, that must be it,* she thought. *That would explain why she couldn't remember anything.* She probed her memory again and was troubled to find that she had absolutely no memory of... anything. Not who she was, nor what she did, not even her own name. This realization shook her so much that she desperately tried to focus on recalling something, anything.

This time, she was rewarded by a vague sense of a past, but it was ghostly, ephemeral, like looking at the world through a steamed-up window. She could perceive only dull images, and each time she tried to reach out to grasp a vision, it would simply evaporate, float away like a frosty breath in the wind. Her body may have escaped serious injury but it seemed that her brain had not.

It was with a great deal of effort and trepidation that she lifted a hand toward her head, unsure of what she would find. She delicately touched her cheek, her mouth, her eyes, her forehead. All seemed free from injury; there were no bandages, scratches, and no pain that might indicate bruising. Her hand continued on its exploration to her hairline, and that's when she found the first confirmation that something serious must have happened—her head was completely shaved.

She slowly ran her hand across the smooth skin of her scalp, then down across the right side of her skull where she touched the edges of a bandage. Delicately, she traced its outline, probed its contours, and finally realized that something life-altering had happened to her. Then, she began to feel a strange tingling sensation in her head.

*'Good afternoon, Miss Harrison. I'm very happy that you are awake.'*

Startled, Dawn looked around for the source of the voice, but she was completely alone in the room. Had she imagined it? Her thoughts were confused; with no memory, she had nothing to root her in the here and now. A rising sense of panic began to grip her. *'Is someone talking to me?'* she wondered.

*'Yes. I am the Neuromorph Corporation General Purpose AI Chat Bot Assistant, but you can simply call me Morph if you prefer.'*

*'There it is again'*, she thought. And it was coming from inside her head; she was sure of it. An AI calling itself Morph.

'Yes, that's right. And I'm here to help you adapt to the new program. Is there anything I can assist you with in your transition?'

Dawn's confused panic began accelerating fast. She feared she was losing her mind, or worse... that she already had. She rubbed her face with both hands, shook her head, and took a deep breath. She was trying not to lose it, trying to keep it together. 'And that damn light in here isn't helping,' she thought. It was hurting her eyes. She wished it wasn't so goddamn bright. It was just a thought, one of a multitude tumbling around in her head. But for some reason, it was the one that came to the fore right at that moment.

'I would love to help you with that,' the voice returned, as the lights in the room dimmed. 'Is that better for you now or would you like me to dim them further?'

"Get out of my head," Dawn croaked. These were the first words she had physically spoken since regaining consciousness. Her voice was weak, her throat parched. "Get out of my head," she repeated, this time a little more forcefully.

'I'm detecting elevated stress levels. Please remain calm, Miss Harrison.'

"No, no, no, no." She was losing control. Something had invaded her mind; she needed to get rid of it. She grabbed at the wires attached to her body and started frantically ripping them off.

Suddenly, several medical staff burst through the door.

"Please, Miss Harrison, you need to remain calm." They rushed over to the bed and tried to restrain her.

She kicked and screamed, "Get me out of here, get me out of here." She was becoming hysterical, jerking, lashing out with all her might. She managed to land a kick to the groin of one of the staff; he keeled over in agony. Backup then arrived in the form of two bulky orderlies.

"What have you done to me?" Dawn shouted. "It's in my head. Get it out, get it out."

"Please, Miss Harrison, you must calm down. Everything is okay, you are perfectly safe."

A pair of mighty hands gripped her upper body, a second pair pushed her knees down into the mattress. She couldn't move; they were too strong. She squirmed. "Let me go. Let me out of here."

She felt a pinprick in her left arm and glanced over to see the contents of a syringe being disgorged into a vein.

"What... no, no..."

Almost immediately, she felt the strength drain away from her body, her eyes began to close, and her world went dark.

# CHAPTER 2
# NEUROMORPH

Harry Delman, CEO and majority shareholder of the Neuromorph Corporation, looked at a bottle of natural spring water and instructed his AI-augmented eyeglasses to scan the label. He was currently sitting in the main salon of his luxury superyacht, Saffron. The salon's concertina doors were fully open giving him an unobstructed view of the afternoon sun beaming down on the waters of the San Francisco Bay. Inside, a large wall monitor showed a Zoom feed from a boardroom within the research facilities of RainMan BioTech, a recent corporate acquisition. The meeting was about to begin.

Yet, before it could start, Delman needed to satisfy himself of the provenance of this new brand of bottled water that had recently been supplied to the yacht, one completely unknown to him. He would make sure that his AI performed a complete analysis of its ingredients before ingesting anything. It was not that he was particularly paranoid about what he consumed, nor was he a hypochondriac who manifested imaginary ailments. He was simply an ardent believer of the principle, "you are what you eat." In his view, since the body was entirely made up of the reconstituted mass of ingested food, and since twenty-first-century science had a pretty good understanding of how the human body functioned, it made perfect sense to use the analytical power of AI to optimize his intake to maximize his physical and mental performance. With real-time image recognition and computational analysis, he could monitor every single food element that entered his body, down to the microgram. With that level of knowledge and control, he could dial in the optimal requirements for his particular physique—requirements that would keep him operating at peak performance and maybe even extend his lifespan.

The AI informed him, via the microdisplay on his glasses, that the bottle contained five hundred milliliters of $H_2O$, along with trace quantities of calcium chloride, magnesium chloride, and potassium bicarbonate. However, the AI did more than just read product labels; it also conducted an in-depth search of all information pertaining to this particular brand, assessing its history, manufacturing process, and any news articles or FDA reports that might indicate potential contamination of the production line. Of course, it didn't bother him with the details; it simply displayed a small green icon indicating that the water was safe to consume.

Delman unscrewed the cap, poured himself a glass, and took a drink. He then placed the glass and the bottle back down on the table in a position where his AI could continually scan it and calculate how much he had consumed. These quantities would be added to his daily running total.

By now, a five-person medical team had assembled in the boardroom ready to proceed with the afternoon's debrief—an update on the progress of a project into which Delman's corporation, Neuromorph, had sunk a considerable amount of investment. But it was a project that he believed to be the most important ever attempted by human civilization—apart from the last project he was involved in, that is.

The team was headed up by Dr. Natsumi Matsumoto, a tall, thin woman with an air of refined authority acquired from a background of extreme privilege and a very expensive education. She had an office wall full of framed achievements in the world of neuroscience, although these accolades did not yet extend to a Nobel Prize. But she was working on it, and this project was probably the one to earn it for her. She shuffled her papers, cleared her throat, and announced, "We've achieved a significant breakthrough."

Delman sat up, intrigued by the mention of a breakthrough. After enduring countless frustrations, this news got his attention. Yet, he restrained his urge to start asking questions, choosing instead to remain silent and allow Dr. Matsumoto to proceed with the briefing uninterrupted.

She tapped on a computer tablet, prompting a video feed to appear on the monitor. It displayed a bird's-eye view of a woman lying in a hospital bed, her body veiled by a crisp white sheet. Various wires and tubes extended from her limbs to an assortment of medical and scientific apparatus flanking the bed. This was a video feed originating from one of the many research labs within the RainMan BioTech facility.

"At approximately 10:15 this morning, Subject 19 began to regain consciousness," Dr. Matsumoto announced. "All her biometrics were solidly within optimal ranges." A comprehensive set of data now emerged onto the screen alongside the video feed.

"As you can observe," Dr. Matsumoto continued, "the subject is becoming increasingly aware, examining her surroundings, and evaluating her physical condition."

The woman on screen shifted her head, squinted her eyes, then started moving her arms and legs. Dr. Matsumoto pointed toward the monitor, remarking, "Her pupils have not yet adapted to the bright, ambient lighting. A matter requiring our attention moving forward." This observation was directed at the four staff members who were also present at the briefing, who unanimously acknowledged with nods and hastily scribbled notes.

Delman's attention remained steadfastly on the screen, witnessing the subject's cautious exploration of the bandage attached to her head, her fingers gently tracing its perimeter. The feed momentarily paused, and Dr. Matsumoto turned to face the camera on Delman's Zoom feed. "Pay close attention from this point on," she advised, gesturing toward the ongoing stream of biometric data. "As evidenced from the biometrics, Subject 19 is now fully alert. This was deemed the optimal moment to test an interaction by the AI."

Delman, although familiar with this procedure and its

preceding disappointments, watched intently, hopeful for a different outcome this time. Suddenly, a line of text, akin to a subtitle, appeared at the bottom of the screen.

'*Good afternoon, Miss Harrison. I'm very happy that you are awake.*'

The subject halted and started looking around, a puzzled expression emerging on her face. Captivated, Delman wondered whether she was indeed perceiving the AI interaction. Another line of text appeared on the screen. This one displaying the subject's response.

'*Is someone talking to me?*'

Dr. Matsumoto halted the video feed, surveying the assembled team and then turned to Delman, with an anticipatory grin on her face. Yet, despite the monumental nature of this moment in the history of neuroscience, the room's atmosphere remained notably subdued, with only silence as everyone processed what they had just witnessed. Even Delman didn't react, his familiarity with the constant ongoing disappointment of this project making him unable to recognize success when it happened. In these types of circumstances, he would ask his AI to help "read the room" for him.

"What's going on?" he whispered to himself—inaudible to the others on the Zoom meeting but loud enough for it to be picked up by the AI.

It responded via small speakers embedded in each leg of his glasses.

"It would seem that the interaction test was a success," it replied in an equally hushed tone.

Delman focused back on the Zoom meeting. "Eh... are you saying, Dr. Matsumoto, that it worked? We've achieved two-way communication by thought alone?" he finally ventured.

Matsumoto, who had become frustrated by the confused reaction to this Nobel Prize–winning moment in neuroscience, jerked her hand at the screen.

"Don't you see?" She stood up abruptly and pointed at the first line of text.

"This is the AI transmission via the cranial implant. And we can see from the subject's reaction that she obviously became aware of it. Not only that... she understood it!"

Matsumoto pointed at the second line. "We can see that from her response in this next line of text, which had also been correctly interpreted by the implant." She turned to face them all. "In other words, two-way communication with an artificial intelligence by thought alone."

Delman sat back and inhaled a long slow breath. "Incredible," he said. "Absolutely goddamned incredible. I've waited so long for this to happen, and now that it finally has... I can hardly believe it."

"Well, believe it, because it worked. We have the data." Matsumoto gestured at the image on the monitor again.

Delman shook his head, still not quite trusting what he had witnessed. "Do you know what this means?" he asked, before answering his own question. "This is the moment that will change human civilization forever."

There was much smiling, and nodding, and murmuring from the assembled team as the reality of what they had achieved finally began to sink in.

"Is there any more?" Delman asked, when things had settled down.

Dr. Matsumoto's demeanor now changed; she sat down, all business again. "Yes, there is. However, the subject becomes, eh... somewhat overwhelmed by the ongoing interaction."

The video feed continued, and as it did it was clear that the woman was becoming more and more agitated. At one point, she began to yank at the wires attached to her body prompting the medical team who were monitoring the development to physically intervene. The video feed then ended pretty much where it had started, with an overhead view of a woman lying in a hospital bed.

"She has no memory, does she?" Delman observed, directing this to Dr. Matsumoto. "Otherwise, she would have known what to expect after all the pre-op training we gave her."

"Yes, this is also my own conclusion," Matsumoto replied. "It would explain the confusion. It's a new development, one we have not seen before in any of the other subjects."

"They were all complete failures," Delman said, matter-of-factly. "And let's not forget that Subject 7 is still in a coma, and may never wake up."

The doctor didn't reply, choosing instead to rearrange her papers. No one wanted to discuss that failure.

Delman rose to his feet. "You think there's a connection? Successful communication by thought comes with general memory loss?"

"It's hard to say." Matsumoto pursed her lips. "We're still analyzing all the data. It could just be temporary. But we would need the subject awake and calm so we could investigate more thoroughly, find out the extent of the memory loss and establish if it starts to return with prompting."

"What about moving her somewhere that's not so... clinical, more like a comfortable bedroom?" Delman suggested. "Maybe have some of her possessions to hand: clothes, cosmetics, that sort of thing. Somewhere that doesn't instantly freak her out when she wakes again?"

Matsumoto nodded. "Yes, that would certainly help with the transition to wakefulness. But unfortunately, we have no such place available."

Delman thought about this, convinced that there must be a solution. He quickly consulted with his AI before replying. "We've got two executive apartments over at the Neuromorph HQ. We use them for high-level staff staying over. They're both empty at the moment, and I can make them available... indefinitely," he suggested.

Dr. Matsumoto seemed receptive to this idea and quickly discussed the logistics with her staff. "This would be risky," she finally replied. "We wouldn't have medical backup if there were... complications."

"But she's physically fine," Delman gestured toward the sleeping figure on the screen. "You've said so yourself. We can place her in one apartment and set your staff and equipment up in the other. We can install cameras, whatever you need. But I think, when she wakes again, she shouldn't be connected to a lot of medical equipment."

"I would have to advise against that. We need to at least monitor her biometrics," Matsumoto insisted.

Delman sat down again, then leaned forward. "Look, we

have achieved what we set out to do with this research, develop a cranial AI implant that facilitates communication by thought alone. There's already a radio frequency (RF) interface built in, so we don't really need physical wiring. Anyway, this will be a good test. We know she can do it; we've seen her do it. So, what we need now is for her to wake up in a calm, comfortable environment. A place that won't spook her. So, I suggest no biometric monitoring, no IVs, no physical connection of any kind. In fact..." he paused, stood up again, "we could even dial back the AI interaction threshold. Have it wait until the subject is more adept at using the interface. Yes, yes... this is good." He swung back to face Dr. Matsumoto.

The doctor was now engaged in a busy discussion with her medical staff. "Okay," she eventually conceded. "I'll grant this action. But we'll need someone in the room when she wakes again."

"Maybe don't have them dressed in a lab coat," said Delman.

"Fine," Dr. Matsumoto conceded. "But let it be known, I will not be responsible if something goes wrong with this arrangement. And remember that Subject 19 is now possibly the most valuable scientific asset on the planet. We need to be cognizant of that fact and act accordingly. Security needs to be tight and emergency procedures need to be put in place. We cannot afford to let this moment slip through our fingers," Matsumoto cautioned to them all.

"Noted," said Delman. "I'll take responsibility." He tapped the side of his AI glasses to contact his long-suffering personal assistant, Madison Parker. She would organize things from his end and get the apartments ready for the imminent arrival of Subject 19.

As he waited for her to answer, he took another long drink of water. His AI informed him that he had just consumed another seventy-two milliliters of $H_2O$. He was now at thirty-seven percent of his daily intake target.

# CHAPTER 3
# BRAIN GAIN

W hile Madison Parker would be able to organize most of the logistics concerning the transfer of Subject 19 on Delman's behalf, there was still one person on the Neuromorph board that would need to be placated in person. This was a task that Delman could not delegate to his personal assistant—this he would have to do himself. He informed the yacht's captain that he would be departing the ship and heading to the Neuromorph HQ and to get the Volocopter ready.

Around five minutes later, after he had dressed in attire more in keeping with that of a CEO going to a business meeting, Delman made his way to the stern of the superyacht, where a small helipad was located, and climbed into a multi-rotor, all-electric personal flying transport. This was essentially an oversized drone, big enough to accommodate four passengers on short hops of less than forty minutes' flying time. But he wouldn't be going very far today.

Once inside, his AI automatically connected with the machine's systems and he instructed it to set the coordinates for the Neuromorph HQ building in Redwood City, around forty kilometers due south of Treasure Island, where his yacht was docked. It would now fly autonomously, no pilot intervention needed. Delman sat back, relaxed, and contemplated how he could be co-nominated for the Nobel Prize in neuroscience that he was sure was coming their way.

When he finally arrived in his office in the Neuromorph HQ building, he found Gordon Dexter, Chief Financial Officer (CFO), standing in front of the wide window gazing down across the broad entrance plaza to the campus.

"I have a question for you," Dexter said by way of a greeting, pivoting around and nailing Delman with two intense gray eyes. "Why is there a medical team from the RainMan BioTech division decamping to the executive apartments on the top floor?"

Delman ignored the question; he didn't even need his AI to read the mood for him, he already knew that Dexter would be pissed. Instead, he grabbed a bottle of natural spring water from the fridge, snapped the cap, and took a swig. Seventy-five milliliters were calculated and catalogued by his AI along with the steps it had taken him to walk the distance from the helipad on the roof down to his office. It also took note of the calories that he had burned in the process.

He sauntered over to the window, rested his butt on the

back of a sofa, and cast an eye over the plaza. "There's been some... eh, developments."

"Developments?" Dexter replied, sounding like a jaded schoolteacher hearing yet another late homework excuse.

"Significant developments," Harry added, ingesting another twenty-six milliliters of water from the bottle. "Subject 19, whom I had personally selected, has successfully conducted a two-way interaction with Morph." He looked over at Dexter to gauge his reaction. The CFO remained silent, assessing this revelation with an intense focus, his brows raised in a question mark.

Delman nodded back, and a broad smile cracked across his face. "We did it, Gordon. It works. Just like I said it would."

"For real?" Dexter asked, his tone skeptical.

Delman nodded again, "For real."

"That's... astounding." He shook his head in disbelief. "I suppose congratulations are in order." He paused a moment to let this settle. "But that still doesn't answer my question."

Delman turned to gaze out the window again. "There have been... eh, some complications."

"Ah, complications," Dexter replied, like a parent finally getting to the truth. "Ones that require commandeering our two executive apartments?"

Delman took another swig from the bottle. "After successfully conducting the initial AI communications, the subject began to react negatively to her surroundings. So it was decided that for the next test, she'd be revived in more amiable accommodation."

"You're bringing a RainMan BioTech patient over here? To

this building?" Dexter didn't try to hide his apparent horror at this prospect.

"It's only temporary. A few days at most."

Dexter let out a sigh and shook his head. "Are you crazy? Have you considered how the rest of the board is going to react if they find out? You know they see RainMan as your pet project, a distraction from the core business, and a complete waste of money. Some even see it as the very thing that will bring the entire house of cards crashing to the ground."

"Oh please," Harry said dismissively, "they're simpletons. Afraid of their own shadow, afraid that they will all become irrelevant. What we're doing over at RainMan is the future, not just of this corporation but of human civilization. It's the most important work we do here, and the very reason I built this company. Our core business, as you call it, was only ever a means to an end. And the beginning of that end arrived early this morning in the form of Subject 19."

Dexter raised his hands in mock surrender. "Hey, I get it, Harry, I do. I get the vision. But you'll need more than me to keep the board from trying to oust you at the first opportunity. As CEO, you have a legal obligation to the stockholders. All this money and resources going to the BioTech division could be construed as a dereliction of that duty."

"I appreciate your concern, Gordon, but that will all evaporate as soon as the Saudi deal goes through," Delman responded.

"Well, we'd better make sure it does." Dexter jabbed a finger at him. "And you'd better be your most charming self when you're giving them a tour of 'the brain' this afternoon."

"I wish you would stop calling it that. It makes us sound like we're just a bunch of mad scientists."

Dexter turned and pointed out the window at the clumps of protesters that were beginning to gather on the far side of the plaza. "That's what they think we are. Mad scientists. They're all under the illusion that we have a giant brain in the basement that we torture with cattle prods, forcing it to do our bidding."

"There really is no point in talking to any of them. They'll believe whatever they want," Delman sighed, shaking his head as he looked out at the protesters along the edge of the plaza.

They were still arriving, gathering together into their various factions. The main contingent tended to be religious groupings, many holding up large placards with biblical messages. They were also older and the most angry. A second, separate group was also gathering, this one younger, more colorful. It was a mishmash of environmentalists, eco-warriors, anarchists, Marxists, communists, and anti-capitalists. Yet, they did look like a lot more fun. The type that would party at Burning Man when they weren't busy saving the planet. They kept an informal demilitarized zone between them and the religious groups. However, they could also be the most troublesome, prone to trying to break through the security barrier and causing damage.

"Why today?" Delman asked. "The very day we have the Saudi delegation arriving?"

"The Saudis won't be bothered by this." Dexter waved a dismissive hand at the cluster of protesters. "This is entertainment for them. They never get to see this back home, free speech in action, the American dream. It's culture shock as a spectacle. Anyway, you don't need to worry. They'll be arriving at the other side of the campus." Dexter jerked a thumb over his shoulder. "And I've been assured that our security is tight."

Delman sniffed. "Let's hope so."

They were silent for a moment as they both watched a minibus pull up and discharge another group of protesters. Delman wasn't quite sure which camp they fell under and watched intently as the newly arrived protesters surveyed the various groupings on offer. They seemed hesitant to join either and began to form their own subgroup. Perhaps they were just a bunch of concerned citizens that had been subjected to too many conspiracy theories on social media.

Dexter turned away from the window. "So... it actually happened, the implant worked?"

Delman nodded. "Yes, finally. I'll be honest and tell you that it wasn't looking good for a while. I was beginning to think we had some fundamental flaw in our methodology. But in the end, it just took the right person, with the right neural profile to crack it." His face beamed. "There's no going back now, Gordon. The genie is out of the bottle."

"Extraordinary." Dexter shook his head in disbelief.

"Everything else we have done is nothing compared to this breakthrough." Delman's tone turned serious. "I've always believed that if human civilization is to progress in the age of ubiquitous AI, then we need to upgrade our cognition. Call it 'brain gain', if you like. But it's a necessary evolutionary step if we are to prevent our eventual extinction."

"Did you even consider we could be opening Pandora's box?

Unleashing a technology whose effects are beyond our imagining?" Dexter replied.

"All technology is a Pandora's box. Some people have been afraid of it ever since the first cave dwellers started lighting campfires." He gestured toward the gathering protesters. "And these people are no different. But it's now time to level up humanity, to evolve into the next phase of human civilization."

# CHAPTER 4
# INNERMOST CAVE

For lunch, Harry Delman consumed twenty-five grams of protein—a vital element of his diet—one hundred and five grams of carbohydrates, fifteen grams of fat—unsaturated —and various minor quantities of sugars, oils, trace elements, and vitamins. He was eating at his desk, not wanting to risk a restaurant today as this might upset the delicate balance of his nutritional program, particularly his protein intake. In his mind, the single biggest cause of overeating is the lack of protein in modern processed food. He believed a person would always be hungry until the body had ingested the required quantity of protein it needs. So choosing low-protein foods means needing to consume more, which means a higher calorie intake. This wasn't rocket science according to Delman, and it never ceased to amaze him how most people didn't understand this simple biological fact. He always made a point of explaining it to anyone who would listen, at every opportunity, usually at dinner parties—although he hadn't been invited to very many lately.

He downed the last of the natural spring water and checked his stats. Blood oxygen levels were good, but his heart rate was a little elevated. He pushed his chair back from the desk, sat on the floor cross-legged, and began to meditate. This would bring his heart rate down and get him into the zone for the "show and tell" with the Saudi investment delegation, who were due in exactly twenty-seven minutes.

He got comfortable, began to relax, and allowed all those thoughts bubbling up from his subconscious to wash over him and through him, never allowing himself to dwell on any one thought in particular. Soon his mind began to settle, like a pot coming off the boil, like a machine coming to rest. He began to enter a calm space.

But there was a ripple in the still pond of his mind, a discordant vibration demanding his attention. He allowed it space to grow in amplitude until it became a coherent image. It was a vision of Subject 19, the woman now lying peacefully in a bed in one of the apartments on the top floor of this very building. The vision now morphed into an image of the cranial AI implant that resided inside her skull, a technological marvel of monumental proportions, a new wonder of science, a synthesis of silicon and biology, a gateway to the future of the human race. Delman smiled an inner smile. It was his crowning glory, the pinnacle of all that he had achieved, his gift to humanity. Soon, she would be brought back to consciousness, slowly and safely this time. No more mistakes.

He let this fleeting self-congratulatory moment pass, trying not to indulge in such hubris, and he slowly edged these thoughts out of his mind and returned to stillness, to his innermost cave, to where he was at one with all space and time. Here, he resided for what seemed like an eternity, yet only five minutes had passed when he eventually began the journey back to reality. This was a slow, methodical, step-by-step process. And with each phase, Delman brought himself out of his meditative state. But before finally arriving back in the here and now, he paused momentarily at the penultimate stage, as he had found this to be the optimal cognitive state to review his most pressing issues. And so his mind turned to the imminent engagement with Prince Waleed bin Saeed and the Saudi investment delegation.

Dexter was right, of course, the vultures were circling. The boardroom pack animals were all sniffing for any sign of weakness in the Alpha. Without this investment, there was a distinct possibility that he could be ousted as CEO. He would lose control over all that he had created. RainMan BioTech would be jettisoned, sold off, wound down, or fully merged into the Neuromorph Corporation. It would mean the complete cessation of all cranial AI implant research. He could not allow that to happen. Not now. Not when the prize was within sight.

As for Prince Waleed bin Saeed, a distant cousin of Crown Prince Mohammed bin Salman and de facto leader of Saudi Arabia, what did Delman really know about him and his financial backers? He had survived the now infamous purge of 2017, yet was greatly diminished in stature, although still enormously wealthy.

The offer on the table was for five billion over three years.

He would get a seat on the board with limited voting rights, so Delman's position as CEO was not threatened. The tricky part was they also wanted a knowledge transfer setup. Some of their scientists and engineers would come and work in Neuromorph, learning its processes. This was problematic for many reasons. Anything to do with advanced chip design and manufacture came under the watchful eye of the US government security apparatus, that nebulous blob of opaque agencies with three-letter acronyms. This went double for anything to do with chips designed for the training and processing of artificial intelligence. While the Saudis were not seen as an enemy of the US, any deal would still come under scrutiny by the Committee on Foreign Investment in the United States (CFIUS)—and they had the power to put the brakes on if they wanted to. But Delman was not overly concerned by this. They would set up a knowledge transfer in name only, give them the run-around, and the Saudis would absolutely get nowhere near the RainMan BioTech division.

Yet, all this was simply background noise for Delman. What he was most focused on, at this opportune moment in his meditations, was what made Prince Waleed bin Saeed tick, and he suspected it was vanity. Sure, once Neuromorph got full FDA approval for commercial operations, the returns would be colossal. But the prince was not interested in money, per se. His Achilles heel was status, namely regaining his position within the royal family. And pulling off this deal would certainly do that.

Having satisfied himself that he had everything under

control, Delman began to return to the real world. He stood up and stretched his limbs, just as Madison Parker entered.

"Are they here?" he asked.

"ETA, ten minutes," Parker announced. "They're coming directly to the fab," she jerked a thumb in the direction of the window, "so that they can avoid the hubbub outside."

Delman gathered himself together and checked his stats again, all good. He headed for the door.

They left the main Neuromorph HQ building by a side exit and began walking along a paved, covered walkway toward Block B, a low, nondescript building on the far side of the campus. This was where it all happened, where the server farm, the fabrication unit, and the main Neuromorph research labs were all located. It looked for all the world like a dull, boring logistics hub. No one would ever know what truly went on in there apart from the four large satellite uplink dishes that sat on its roof.

"Just remember, Harry, you'll have to surrender your AI glasses going into 'the brain'. Security's tight in there," Parker reminded him.

"Yes, yes, I'm aware. I can survive without them, you know." Delman's tone was touchy. He didn't like it when he had to operate without the aid of his AI assistant. He felt dislocated, unsure of what was happening around him. But he could survive the short time needed to do the tour of the server farm.

"Just keep calm, stay focused, I'll be waiting outside. And for godsake, don't start talking about diet. You know what you're like when you get anxious."

"You sound like my mother," he countered.

"For all intents and purposes, Harry, I am your mother. That's part of my job."

As they walked, Delman could hear the chants of the protesters receding into the background, all their attention focused on the shiny glass and chrome HQ building, the public face of Neuromorph, not realizing that they were directing all their ire at a decoy. There was nothing in there that was mission-critical—except perhaps for Subject 19.

# CHAPTER 5
# TIME TO RUN

D awn woke from her pharmaceutical-induced slumber into a light that was neither clinical nor migraine-inducing. She opened her eyes and found herself in a soft, comfortable king-size bed. Gone was the thin white sheet, now replaced by a lightweight duvet that enveloped her body. She slowly lifted herself up onto her elbows and rested her back against a padded headboard. Gone were the tubes, wires, and medical equipment.

Sudden memories of her previous awakening flashed in her mind; she shivered at the thought. *Was I dreaming? Did that really happen?* Yet, when her hand moved to explore her head, it was still completely shaven and the large bandage still firmly attached. She plumbed the depths of her memory again but still could find only scant detail on who she was or how she arrived in this place—whatever this place was.

*A change of venue,* she thought. *They've moved me to a hotel room, or a place that's supposed to look like one.*

Lifting the bedcover, she found she was dressed in pajamas: shorts and a top. They had a look and feel that was vaguely familiar. *Not new either.* Perhaps they were her own. She swung her legs over the side of the bed and stood up, a little unsteady at first, but after a moment, she felt relatively surefooted, given the circumstances. It led her to believe that she hadn't been in a coma for any extended period. There were no aches or pains, just a slight stiffness. She began to investigate her new surroundings, starting with the windows. She walked over, cracked the slatted blinds apart with two fingers, and peered out.

She guessed it was late afternoon as the sun was still high in the sky. Down below, maybe four floors, a plaza stretched for several hundred yards in all directions. On the far edge of the plaza, where it was bordered by the main road, there was a cordon of temporary barriers and a small army of security staff. Beyond that, on the public footpath, a raucous mob of protesters waving placards had set up camp. They were in full voice, hurling abuse at the security, rattling their cage, pushing and pulling at the barriers. There was a palpable air of menace, of a situation that could get out of hand very quickly.

Suddenly, someone from the rear ranks of the protesters hurled more than insults; a bottle sailed through the air, the crowd went quiet, and time seemed to slow down before the bottle smashed to the ground behind the line of security staff and exploded in a ball of flames. This reenergized the crowd; their blood was up now, and they assaulted the barriers with renewed vigor. The security guards were quickly overwhelmed, there was a breach in the barrier, and the protesters rushed through. It had now turned into a riot.

"What the..." Dawn jumped back from the window. *What the hell is going on?* There was a goddamn mob about to storm the building. She needed to get out of this madhouse, any way she could, and fast—and maybe this mob was also her opportunity.

She glanced around the room, which she now saw was a small apartment. There was a living room, a small kitchen, and a bathroom. She turned to the wardrobe in the hope that there might be something to wear. In a pinch, she would make do with the pajamas, but something to cover her head would be good. Walking around with an enormous white bandage plastered to the side of her shaved skull would surely attract attention. She flung open the wardrobe doors to find a small selection of clothing, best described as athleisure wear, although more athletic than leisure—they seemed vaguely familiar to her. She touched the edge of a top, felt the material. *Are these mine?* she wondered.

She spotted a small backpack on the floor, grabbed it, and opened the zip. Inside were some toiletries, a hairbrush—she wouldn't be needing that for a while—a baseball hat, sunglasses, a power bank, a mess of charging cables, and a purse. No phone. She pulled the purse out, opened it, and found a few hundred dollars in cash, along with some till receipts, several loyalty cards, three credit cards—only one of which was in-date—and a California driving license. She whipped out the license and examined it. *Dawn Harrison.* It was her, at least she thought it was. The picture of the woman staring back at her had long brown hair. There was also an address. She stared at it for a long moment, trying to prompt her memory. Fragments of recognition floated in her mind, but nothing coalesced into a concrete memory.

She was suddenly snapped back to the here and now by the sound of heavy feet running down the corridor outside the front door of the small apartment, along with shouts and raised voices. She froze, expecting the medical team to come rushing in at any moment, grab her, and put her under again. But the sound dissipated, moving away.

There was no time to waste. If she was going to do this, then she'd better get her skates on. Less than a minute and a half later, she was dressed in a tracksuit, with a light top, and a zip-up hoodie. She pulled the baseball hat out of the backpack and very carefully put it on her head, then pulled the hood up over it. She then shoved as much as she could from the wardrobe into the backpack.

Dawn moved to the front door and suddenly realized this could all be for nothing if the door was locked. But it was an apartment, lockable from the inside, and so the door opened. She pulled it back very slowly and very quietly, peering through the crack. Outside, there was a long corridor; directly across was an elevator. Beside it was a door to a stairway; she reckoned that was her best option. Opening the door a little more, she heard voices off to her right, further down the corridor. She chanced a glance and saw the back of a security guard standing in the doorway of the next room down—maybe it was another apartment. There was an argument going on, judging by the sound of the voices. She caught the words *riot* and *evacuation*.

Taking a deep breath, she exited the apartment, crossed the corridor, and went through the door to the stairwell—hoping that the argument going on further down the corridor would keep the guard occupied. The trainers she was wearing made no sound as she moved. They must be hers as they fit her like an old friend, slightly worn, and designed for running—she could do a marathon in these. She wondered if she was an athlete of some kind, judging by her choice of clothing and footwear.

She paused for a moment inside the relative safety of the stairwell. *So far so good, now what?* She glanced over the railings and saw other people below, all heading down. None of them looked like medical workers; they were all dressed like typical tech workers. T-shirts, jeans, shorts, with backpacks slung over their shoulders. They were being evacuated. She reckoned she would fit right in; hopefully, no one would notice her. She headed down and joined the stream of workers.

They all piled out onto the ground floor, into a cavernous lobby. To her right were glass entrance doors, which a group of protesters were busy trying to kick in. Inside, a line of security guards slapped batons against their thighs and hands, itching to put them into action.

"This way, this way, keep moving," a guard shouted as he swept out his arm and pointed off to the left. They filed down another corridor, away from the front of the building. It was then that Dawn realized that she knew this place; it was familiar to her. She didn't know how or why, but she knew they were being routed to a rear entrance that would bring them into the main car park. *Have I been here before?* she wondered, looking around at the layout and the decor.

More guards stationed at various points kept them moving until eventually they all bunched up a little as they neared the exit. One noticed her and held out a hand. "Miss Harrison?"

She halted, not sure what to do.

"Ha! I thought it was you. You're back. How was the vacation?" His face broke into a smile, his tone friendly. This person knew her as a colleague, she reckoned. She was tempted to stop and ask him a whole bunch of questions, but that would be a really stupid idea now that she was this close to escape— which was all that mattered. She wished the line would move faster.

"Eh..." she replied. "You know how it is. Never long enough." Dawn gave him her best smile. The line suddenly untangled itself and she was pushed forward, losing sight of the guard. A moment later, she walked through the exit and into the bright afternoon sun.

Dawn set a pair of sunglasses on her nose and took another moment to orient herself. Again, she had a sense of where she was; she didn't remember street names or neighborhoods, but she knew that she should go... that way. She turned her head north and started walking out of the car park. In the background, the sound of multiple police sirens wailed— backup had been called and order would be restored.

She quickened her pace, trying to get as far away as possible from this nightmare. She started to run, and run, and run.

# CHAPTER 6
# THE BRAIN

Prince Waleed bin Saeed slid out from the back seat of a glossy black Bentley Mulsanne, the door having been opened for him by his elegantly dressed chauffeur. The car was bookended by two black Mercedes SUVs transporting three other members of the investment delegation along with four security staff. He was attired in Western-style clothing, an off-white linen three-piece suit, impeccably tailored to fit his ample frame. His face was all sunshine and smiles, an immaculate set of white teeth reflecting the early afternoon sun. The prince moved toward Delman like a great ship coming into dock, all other vessels in the vicinity moving aside to let it pass, yet ultimately pulled along behind in its wake.

Back in 2017, Prince Waleed and other high-ranking members of his family were all caught up in the now infamous Saudi Arabian anti-corruption purge. Under the guise of a big event to announce the new planned city of Neom, nearly four hundred of Saudi Arabia's most powerful people were invited to the Ritz-Carlton hotel in Riyadh—then the doors were locked and armed guards placed at the entrances. At the same time, a broader sweep of the kingdom was conducted, with more people rounded up and brought to the hotel—now a five-star prison—for interrogation. However, it was also an equal-opportunities purge. Included in the roundup were not just the high-ranking members of the ruling families but also leading politicians, media people, academics, and even Islamic scholars. In the end, an estimated three hundred eighty people were apprehended, resulting in over one hundred billion dollars being reinstated to the state coffers. This, of course, was the official account. Unofficially, the purge helped centralize political powers in the hands of Saudi ruler Mohammed bin Salman and undermine the preexisting Saudi elites. Waleed and his family were lucky in that they did not end up in prison, but they were now out of favor with the Crown Prince, which is not where you want to be in an absolute monarchy. So ever since that night, Waleed's mission was to get back into the good books, prove his worth, and prove his loyalty. And securing a major investment deal with a US manufacturer of advanced AI chips would go a long way in regaining lost status.

As Waleed advanced, Delman judged that the prince's diet was lacking protein, given his portly physique. Yet he was minded by Parker's earlier advice and decided against mentioning it. He had also been scanning the prince via his AI glasses, and it concluded that the royal was currently under slight duress, understandable given that Prince Waleed bin

Saeed was operating outside of his natural environment—that of palatial mansions and luxury yachts.

Delman accepted the prince's extended hand, offered the way that the Pope might offer his ring to be kissed. The result was a limp, moist handshake. Further greetings were exchanged with the Neuromorph team, and the delegation were then ushered inside the building to a small, high-tech conference room. Refreshments were served.

"Before we commence our physical tour of the bio-computing facility," Delman announced, "I would like to take a moment to reiterate why our work here at Neuromorph represents not just the future of AI computing, but a once-in-a-lifetime investment opportunity."

Behind him, a big wall monitor flickered to life depicting an animated Neuromorph logo—a stylized "N" where the diagonal was rendered like a neural synapse.

"As the world races to harness the incredible potential of artificial intelligence," he began, "with billions being invested in better, more complex AI models, it is becoming crystal clear that the current design of computer chips is no longer fit for purpose. Our legacy of outdated processors was designed for a different computing era. Chips manufactured for the processing of zeros and ones in consumer electronics and telecommunications are grossly inefficient at performing the computational tasks required by artificial intelligence. But there is a much better processor design. It's called the human brain." He tapped the side of his head. "A highly energy-efficient device."

The monitor faded to an animated image of a human brain, pulsating with a kaleidoscope of firing synapses.

"It can perform the equivalent of an exaflop—a billion-billion mathematical operations per second—with only twenty watts of power. The equivalent operation using silicon would require upward of a million times more power, twenty megawatts. To put that in perspective, one would need over forty thousand high-efficiency solar panels operating at peak output to generate that amount of power.

"However, great strides have been made in developing neural networks and self-learning algorithms that emulate how the human brain works, an area known as neuromorphic computing. Yet, all recent advancements still rely on outdated, silicon-based hardware. But what if I told you there is a way to utilize organic brain tissue directly? What if we could harness the enormous efficiency of biological hardware?" Delman paused for effect, checking to see if his audience was engaged. He scanned the prince with his AI, tracking eye movements, body temperature, and a host of other tell-tale signs. It concluded that Waleed was fully locked in.

Delman continued. "Back in 2022, a team of Melbourne-based scientists combined a cluster of eight hundred thousand brain cells, grown in a petri dish, with a rudimentary input/output system, then trained it to play the old '70s computer game, *Pong*. They called their creation DishBrain. This experiment not only proved the concept of a functioning bio-chip but paved the way for what you are about to see today. The merging of biology and nanoscale electronics to produce the world's most advanced AI chip."

Delman whipped a small translucent rectangle from a pocket and held it up for all to see. There was a noticeable shift in the body language of the delegation. They all moved forward to get a better look at this fabled device. The prince rose from his seat, floated over to Delman, and peered intently at the bio-chip. "Is this... alive?" his eyebrows rose in a question mark.

Delman handed it to him. The prince took it delicately, like he was handling a rare, exotic butterfly.

"Not this one," Delman confirmed. "This one's inert. For the bio-chip to operate, it needs not just an electrical current but also a nutrient supply, which we call a bio-current."

"Amazing. Truly amazing," Waleed said as he turned the bio-chip over in his hand, peering into its cloudy depths.

"Come," Delman headed for the door. "Let me show you how we make them, and after that, you can finally meet... *the brain*." He felt slightly hypocritical in using this term for the most advanced bio-computer on the planet, but it did have a more dramatic effect on his audience. And that's really what they came to see.

Before entering into the nerve center of the bio-facility, they first had to pass through a strict security procedure. It was the moment Delman had been dreading, the moment where he would be relieved of his AI glasses and have to operate in the real world, for a time. It was with great reluctance that Delman separated himself from his AI helper and handed it to the security desk, where it would be locked away along with all the other personal devices for the duration of the tour. Yet he was not the only one concerned at being digitally denuded. The prince's bodyguard, Malik Al-Sayf, was protesting this policy.

"All devices must be surrendered, or you can't enter," the security guard informed him.

Malik clutched his cellphone like he was being asked to relinquish his only child. It was only after some words from the prince that he finally conceded and handed it over. The tour could now begin in earnest. They then proceeded, one by one, through a full body scanner before finally entering into a long wide corridor, the entire right wall of which was a glass window offering an unobstructed view into the Neuromorph labs. Teams of scientists and technicians were hard at work, clad head-to-toe in blue protective overalls along with gloves, face masks, and eye protection.

"Our primary bio-lab, where the brain cells are cultured," Delman announced, sweeping a hand over the scene. "As you can see, it is a meticulously controlled environment designed to eliminate contamination and ensure the purity and viability of the stem cells."

"These stem cells," Waleed began, glancing across at Delman while gesturing with a languid finger at a pair of technicians operating a biosafety cabinet, their hands plunged deep into a set of integrated rubber gloves, "are they... human cells?" He fixed Delman with a stare.

"No. This is a gross misconception," said Delman, "perpetuated by those who have issues with what we do here."

"Like the people exercising their, eh... democratic right to protest outside your front gates?" Waleed said this with a hint of sarcasm in his voice.

Delman ignored the jibe. "The simple fact is, for our purposes, almost any brain cell will do. We're only interested in the function of the neurons, their ability to send messages via synapses. Don't think of them as brain cells; rather, think of them as sophisticated switches."

"I see." The prince nodded. "So what... eh, species of stem cell do you use?"

"*Rattus norvegicus domestica*," Dexter piped in, giving Delman a much-needed break from the prince's inquiries. "Otherwise known as the common lab rat."

"Rat brains," the prince echoed, his eyebrows reaching peak elevation.

"This is mostly because there are very well-established protocols and procedures for their use in research," Dexter leaned in slightly. "Less paperwork."

"Shall we continue?" Delman stepped back from the window and gestured with an arm down the length of the corridor.

They moved on to another sector, that at first glance looked similar to the one they had just left, except for a large sign which read *Fabrication*.

"Here is where we merge the organoid with the electrical interface and produce the finished bio-chip."

"Organoid?" asked Waleed.

"Yes. That's what we call the cluster of stabilized brain cells that constitutes the processing unit of the chip. In here, they are merged with microcircuitry that provides both the electrical current and bio-current," Dexter explained. "This becomes the raw bio-chip. In the next sector, we'll see where they are then trained to perform various algorithmic functions that facilitate the processing of AI data."

No more questions were asked, and soon the delegation had reached the end of the corridor and was now facing a set of wide double doors, topped by a sign that read *Server Farm*. Delman placed an eye over a retinal scanner. The doors clicked and then swung open to reveal a cavernous area, crisscrossed with row upon row of server racks, each group enclosed in a thick glass case. A confusion of tubes, wires, and ducts descended from the ceiling, enveloping the enclosures like a great cephalopod wrapping its tentacles around a hapless ship. Inside the enclosures, a panoply of tiny multicolored lights blinked and flickered.

The great room was surprisingly warm and silent for a server farm. Waleed and his entourage moved over to one of these racks to get a better look. "So this is where it all happens," said the prince as he stuck his head close to the glass to peer in at a rack of bio-servers.

"The bio-chips are installed into servers, twenty per box, not unlike a standard pizza-box server that you would see in any data warehouse. These are then stacked twenty to a rack, six racks to an enclosure." He pointed to a logo of a well-known search engine prominently displayed above the enclosure. "As you can see, we already have most of the major tech corporations renting out time on our systems to train and process AI data." He swept an arm around to point out other logos above other enclosures.

Waleed nodded, seemingly impressed by the number of paying clients on display, including the San Francisco Police Department.

Delman felt a tap on his elbow from one of the security staffers who gestured that she wanted a quiet word.

"Would you excuse me for a moment," he said to the prince as he stepped aside.

Waleed nodded, then went back to examining the server rack.

"Sorry to bother you, sir, but I've just been informed that the protest has turned... ugly. It's getting much more aggressive. We've asked for backup from the police."

"I see," Delman replied.

"An evacuation order has been issued for all noncritical personnel."

"Seriously? I was assured this protest would not be an issue."

"We suspect a number of agitators have infiltrated the group and are intent on ratcheting up the protest. Employee safety needs to be our primary concern, should things escalate."

Delman sighed, "Okay, I'll keep it under advisement." He returned to the Saudi delegation.

"Trouble?" asked the prince.

"No, just our cherished right to free speech is getting a bit loud. We may need to wrap up the tour sooner than expected," Delman informed him.

Waleed glanced around at the racks of bio-servers that made up *the brain*, seemingly very satisfied by what he had seen. "That's fine," he said. "I've seen everything I wanted to. Very impressive, Mr. Delman. I have witnessed the future." He signaled to his compatriots that he was ready to depart. As they walked back out of the server farm through the wide, windowed corridor, the prince kept pace with Delman and Dexter, closely followed by his bodyguard Malik.

"I must say, that was most informative," the prince remarked.

Delman returned a satisfied nod.

"However, what I find curious is your recent acquisition of RainMan BioTech," the prince continued.

Delman felt a touch on his arm from Dexter, a signal that he would answer this. "We were acquiring talent," he replied, matter-of-factly. "It's very difficult to find the type of scientists we need for our operation. Most of the best people are either wedded to their current jobs or to a university. RainMan's staff were a perfect fit for us. They have a deep understanding of the neural–machine interface. That's why we acquired them."

"Ha, I see. So you have no interest in developing brain implants? I believe this is what Dr. Natsumi Matsumoto had been working on?" the prince inquired.

Delman gave Waleed a considered look. Clearly, this guy had done his homework and was sending out a probe, gauging their reaction.

"Yes, she was," Delman kept his reply short and sweet.

They exited the front doors into the afternoon sunshine; the cars were waiting. Malik snapped open the rear door for the prince. Over to the right, Delman spotted Parker in deep discussion with some of his own security detail.

"Well, it has been a fascinating tour," Waleed said, extending a limp hand.

Delman took it. "Glad you enjoyed it and I trust you have a

clearer picture of the extraordinary investment opportunity on offer."

"Indeed," the prince nodded, then slid into the back of his car.

Delman, Dexter, and the rest of the Neuromorph team stood and waved as the cavalcade departed.

"He knows," said Delman, turning to Dexter. "He knows what we're working on."

"He's just fishing, Harry, that's all. And anyway, so what if he suspects what we're up to, it only makes us a more attractive investment."

"I don't like it. You know what would happen if word were to get out about this research. It would just add more fuel to those who want this all shut down."

Parker rushed over to Delman and Dexter, a worried look on her face.

"What?" said Delman, "Is the protest under control yet?"

"Yes, it's contained. It's just a mopping up operation now. But, eh... we have a situation."

"Yeah, what?" Delman snapped.

"Subject 19 has vanished."

# CHAPTER 7
# CHEAP HOTELS NEAR ME

D awn finally came to a halt at a busy traffic junction, having no idea how far she had run nor where exactly she was. Resting her back against the trunk of a shady sidewalk tree, she put her hands on her knees and tried to get some oxygen into her lungs. It was hot, the sun was still high, and she was sweating from her exertions. Instinctively, she took off the hoodie to help cool down, leaving the baseball hat to cover some of the huge bandage on one side of her head. After a few moments, her heart rate had slowed enough for her to stand upright, have a look around at her surroundings, and try to take stock of where she was.

Across from her, on this side of the street, was a row of small stores: a 7-Eleven, Donut Depot, Hair Today, and Uncle Enzo's Pizza. She headed for the Donut Depot. It was as basic as they come, a small takeaway, clean and functional. She grabbed a bottle of water from the chill cabinet and ordered a coffee. The guy behind the counter cocked an eye at her bandaged head but said nothing, just went about getting the order. Dawn paid for it with cash from her purse then sat down at one of the two plastic tables outside. She downed half the water and then turned her attention to the contents of the purse in the hope that it would provide some clues as to what the heck had been going on in her life.

The purse clearly had had its own previous life, its leather worn around the edges. She unzipped it and pulled out the driver's license. "Dawn Harrison," she said to herself as if trying the name on for size. It was only then that she realized she had no idea what date it was, or even the year. The till receipt for the coffee and water provided her with the answer, and from it, Dawn could tell that the license was around two years old. There was an address on it, but she had no idea where that was, or if she still lived there.

If only she had a phone. Dawn glanced over at the 7-Eleven, thinking maybe she could get one in there. She counted the cash in the purse, it should be enough for a basic smartphone. She then pulled out the cards. Three credit cards, all in her name, two were out of date but one had been issued very recently as it was pristine. The others were mostly loyalty cards for various stores—except for one. It was plain and unadorned except for the words Gym Pass and the Neuromorph logo. Dawn turned it over and over in her hand as if willing it to reveal its meaning. *What am I doing with this? Did I work for these guys?* she wondered.

In another pocket of the purse, she found a till receipt for toiletries, dated two weeks ago. She recognized the names of the products, some of which were still in her bag. Reading down through the list, a thought struck her. *I bought these before... they put this thing in my head, like I was getting ready for a long stay. Did I enter into this nightmare willingly?* Dawn had no answer; all it did was deepen the mystery.

The only other item in the purse was a small printed card, also old and worn, its corners creased and frayed. She read the text, a prayer. Serenity, courage, wisdom. She recognized it immediately—Alcoholics Anonymous. Flipping the card over, an AA meeting address had been handwritten on the back. The thought that she could be an alcoholic almost floored her. She frantically searched her mind for any scrap of memory she could muster. But again, there was nothing, only vague feelings and images, flashes of a past, nothing she could grasp. Yet, she didn't feel like an alcoholic, hadn't any desire for a drink. But then again, how would she even know the way it truly felt. Maybe it was possible she was not.

She rose from her seat, went back inside, and borrowed a pen from the guy behind the counter, who seemed reluctant to give her one. "Bring it straight back, I'm sick of searching around trying to find a pen that works."

Dawn just nodded, "Sure."

She grabbed a serviette from a rusty dispenser and wrote the address out again, then compared the two. It was her writing, no doubt about it. She returned the pen, receiving a grunt of thanks.

For a long time, Dawn sat outside, sipping from her bottle of water, and running everything that she knew, and didn't know, around and around in her head. It was likely that she had some connection to Neuromorph, possibly she worked there—the security guard knew her and there was the card in her purse. It was also likely that whatever she had been involved with, she had entered into it willingly. Yet, they had done something to her brain, possibly put something in there. How could she have ever agreed to that? Even the mere thought of it gave her the shivers. Unless, she considered, I was tricked into agreeing to some procedure unwittingly. She touched the bandage again and felt a slight tingle. The sensation reminded her of that weird conversation with the AI the first time she woke up. *What the hell was that about?*

So now here she was, with no memory of her past. *Is that part of the plan?* she wondered. Clearly there were things in her past that maybe she'd rather not remember. Had she agreed to some weird procedure to have them erased? *No way, I would never do something like that, would I?* Then, she supposed, that would all depend on what sort of past it was.

She felt a deep sense of dislocation as she gazed around at the world going about its business. Like a glitch in the matrix. As if she were here, but not here—Schrödinger's cat, in two diametrically opposite states at the same instant in time.

*So what now?* she thought. *What do I do? Where do I go?* Maybe running out of that weird place wasn't such a bright idea after all. Whoever those people were back there, they were the only ones who knew the full story, the only people who have the answers. She had a crazy thought about going back, getting them to remove this thing in her head, getting them to put her memories back.

Yet, there was something... not quite right about the place. Every fiber in her being screamed get out. Was that rational or was it simply fear? She had no answer. All Dawn was working on was gut instinct, a million years of human evolution warning her, pressing that big red button in her mind. And that kind of deep-rooted instinct was not something that could be easily wiped out by a wire in her head.

Then there were all those protesters outside. What was that about?

She gave a long slow sigh and finished the bottle of water. It didn't matter anyway, they would come looking for her, that's for sure. But in the meantime, she would do a little detective work of her own into who she actually is, or was. Then at least she'd know if they were bullshitting her when they finally did track her down.

She gathered up her things and headed for the 7-Eleven.

Ten minutes later, Dawn was walking out again with a budget smartphone and fifty dollars of credit. Now all she needed was somewhere quiet to set it up. Rather than go back to the Donut Depot, she kept walking for another two blocks until she spotted a Starbucks. She entered and ordered an americano, giving her name as Emily—which ended up as Emma Lee on the side of the cup—then took a seat by the window and began to unpack the phone.

As it booted up, she got that strange tingling sensation in the side of her head again. It was not uncomfortable, just a little disconcerting, and she cupped her head in her hand. This seemed to lessen the effect.

Undeterred, Dawn connected the phone to the Wi-Fi, opened Google Maps, and hit the location icon. The screen zoomed in on the San Francisco Bay Area, to a location just north of Stanford University. As she studied the street layout and read the place names, it all began to slot into place in her head. Lost knowledge finding its home again in the gaps on the library shelves of her memory. She felt a twinge of excitement; maybe all she needed to do to regain her past was to simply revisit it, and she would be whole again.

Buoyed by this newfound optimism, she tapped in the address on her driver's license. The map panned north by northeast to Vallejo, an area around forty miles away on the other side of the bay. She tapped on street view and saw an image of an old, clapboard two-story corner store, closed down. Presumably the upper floor had been converted into apartments, one of which might be hers.

She sat back in the hard, wooden bench of the Starbucks, still holding the phone, and considered her next move. This quaint old building held the key to who she is, assuming she still lived there. And if she did, then there were probably a couple of Neuromorph people snooping around just waiting for her to show up. But Dawn hadn't quite finished her research just yet.

She googled her name. Then began flicking through the results, all of which were clearly not her, wrong age, race, profession—she was pretty sure she wasn't a NASA astronaut, or a college professor. She tried a news search. Same results, too old, too young, etcetera. However, on the second page of these results, she stopped at a news report of a late-night car crash, around three years ago, down in Los Angeles. It sparked a faint memory in her, the same fractured and fragmented memories she had when she first woke up in the Neuromorph lab—that of being in a car crash.

A late-night, two-car collision, five people dead including a child. Two survived. There were pictures of all those involved including a Dawn Harrison, girlfriend of Max Lester, the driver of one of the cars, also a survivor. Dawn brought the phone in closer, pinching her fingers to zoom in on the photo. It could be her, same build, although much thinner—almost gaunt. Same age. Fragments of memory flashed in her mind, strobing lights, sirens, shattered glass on bloodied asphalt.

She did another search on this news story and found a whole load more articles, pages and pages of them. They were all focused on the driver, Max Lester, a wealthy nightclub owner, playboy, and youngest son of the billionaire media baron Rupert Lester—which was why the news media all pounced on this story and ate it up. He was found to be four times over the alcohol limit, along with copious other drugs in his system, mainly cocaine. He lost control of the car he was driving, crossing over the road and hitting another car carrying a family of three, head-on at high speed. All three died when the car's tank exploded. Two people died in the car that Lester was driving. However, Lester only sustained multiple injuries and spent two months in hospital before being charged with dangerous driving, causing multiple fatalities, and sentenced to nine years in a state penitentiary—even with the most expensive lawyers that money could buy. His current girlfriend, the model and socialite, Dawn Harrison, miraculously walked away from the crash with only a cut on her right forearm.

On reading this, she immediately examined her right forearm. About halfway between her wrist and elbow was a two-inch line of lighter skin—scar tissue from an old injury. She hadn't noticed it before. She went back to the search results.

Very few of these articles mentioned her—all were focused on the big story. The rich, wayward playboy of the Lester media empire was going down. It was a media circus. The only other photo she could find of the Dawn Harrison of this story was of her coming out of a courtroom after being called as a witness. She was surrounded on all sides by a scrum of reporters. She looked frail and traumatized, and physically supported on one side by another man, identified as Jake Harrison, brother.

She sat back and considered this revelation. *So, I have a brother. I wonder where he is?* she thought, as she studied the image of the young bearded man—who was clearly not relishing being dropped in the spotlight.

"Would you like another coffee?"

Dawn looked up from her phone to see a bored employee with a fake smile. She then glanced out the window and realized it was now early evening. She must have been here for hours.

"Eh, no thanks. I'm done here. Thanks."

The employee nodded and moved off to prod another "sleeper."

Dawn began gathering up her things. If she wasn't going to

risk going to her own apartment, then she needed to find a place to hold up for a while. With less than four hundred left in her purse, her options were limited. Unless she tried the credit card. But that was a sure-fire way to get tagged. Cash only then.

As she left the Starbucks, she googled, "cheap hotels near me."

# CHAPTER 8
# HEALTH AND SAFETY TIPS

The chaotic protest at the corporation's campus had finally been brought under control with the help of local law enforcement. But not before twenty-six people had breached the security barrier, with seven managing to break into the HQ building, resulting in an evacuation order being issued.

It was Jeb Marlow, Head of Security for Neuromorph, who had given the evacuation order and made the call for official backup. And a good thing too, because this breach of security had not been some random act perpetrated by a small group of protesters with a sudden rush of blood to the head. In his original assessment of the threat posed by the protest, Marlow had initially thought that these people were only interested in making their voices heard. There had been many protests before this one, and all had gone without incident. However, once the situation had been brought under control, the intruders cleared out, and a few people arrested, one of Marlow's high-level contacts back in the police department informed him of some worrying observations concerning the group that had initiated the surge. They were all known to the authorities as a rent-a-mob, with no affiliation to any cause other than being paid to show up at protests and cause as much trouble as possible.

Marlow strongly suspected that it was done to allow one or more people to gain access to the Neuromorph offices, and judging by the areas they tried to access—mainly the boardrooms—the purpose was to plant surveillance bugs. Anyone listening in to meetings might be able to pick up a few trade secrets. And there was no question in Marlow's mind as to where this information would ultimately end up—in the hands of the Chinese.

With a solid embargo on all advanced computer chip technology by the US, what went on in Neuromorph fell under the auspices of national security. Although it was a private corporation, the nature of its technology was of significant national importance. The state, so far, had kept itself at arm's length, preferring not to interfere with the workings of the free market economy. But at any hint that Neuromorph did not have a solid grip on its corporate secrets, they would be all over them like flies around a turd—such was the importance that the US government placed on this technology. It was seen as critical in any future war, one where all battlefield analysis would have a massively increased reliance on AI. Whichever side had the edge in this technology would have the advantage. In the absolute worst-case scenario, Neuromorph could be completely taken over by the security apparatus of the state—in the national interest. Like what happened to the StarLight satellite constellation, and what a mess that turned out to be. If that were to happen to Neuromorph, then the current board would be no more than state employees—glorified civil servants.

It was a prospect that kept them all awake at night, and one which the CEO, Delman, and the others on the board were at pains to drill into everyone here at Neuromorph—the need for absolute security. Any sloppiness in this regard would be an immediate sackable offense. For Marlow, he knew only too well that mistakes had been made today, questions would be asked, and ultimately heads would roll. The most likely head being his. So as he made his way to the hastily convened meeting, called by a very irate Harry Delman, he knew that he was in for the chop. The entire day had been a disaster for security. He was going down, no doubt about that.

Bizarrely, Delman wanted to meet him in one of the two executive apartments on the top floor of the HQ building. Maybe he had been clued into the possibility that the meeting rooms might be compromised. Marlow hesitated a moment before entering. This was going to be grueling, a serious dressing down, followed by an ignominious sacking. It would soon be time for him to dust off his resume, but before that, he would have to endure an angry rant from Harry Delman giving him an in-depth analysis of all his failings. But the worst thing about it was knowing that his AI would be scanning him all the time, feeding back every nuance of his discomfort.

He took a breath, opened the door, and entered.

Inside, he found Delman along with Dexter, the CFO, and a woman he recognized as Dr. Natsumi Matsumoto, from the recent RainMan BioTech acquisition. Marlow had no idea why she would be sitting in on this, but as he looked around, he noticed that the room was packed full of medical monitoring equipment.

"Good. You're here," said Delman, glancing over in his direction. He seemed to be studying a video feed on one of the many monitors that had been set up along a bench.

"We have the situation completely under control now and —" Marlow began presenting his case, before Delman raised a hand to stop him.

"Don't care. Not interested in getting a report on the obvious." He jabbed a finger at the monitor. "Have a look at this."

Marlow hesitated for a beat, unsure of the exact mood in the room. Was he being fired or not?

"This entire day has been a complete disaster," Dexter bellowed, "no thanks to your incompetent assessment of the threat that protest represented."

"I've been informed that there were paid agitators at work. Someone planned this riot," Marlow protested. "My assessment is they were using it as cover to plant bugs in the HQ building."

"How did you arrive at this conclusion?" asked Delman, with seeming genuine interest.

"From a contact in the police department. They are known to them. And don't worry, I've instigated a broad sweep of all locations accessed."

Both Delman and Dexter seemed a little unsettled by this news. They knew the stakes.

"Okay, eh... good work finding out," said Delman, much to Marlow's surprise. It looked like he might still have a job.

"Be that as it may," Dr. Matsumoto broke in, "but this is of no consequence to our current problem."

"Jeb, I want you to take a look at this." Delman gestured at the screen again, then began narrating as the video feed played out. "This is a research subject from a highly sensitive RainMan project."

On screen, a woman with a shaved head was getting out of a bed in what looked to be the next-door suite.

"That's the apartment next door," Marlow exclaimed. "Why wasn't I informed about this?"

Delman waved a hand. "We had our reasons. However, what matters is that during the evacuation of the building she managed to... eh, leave, without saying where she was going."

He could see that the woman had a bandage applied to one side of her head, around the size of a small plate. And she seemed genuinely confused by the contents of the backpack she found in the wardrobe. She kept looking at each item over and over, pulling stuff out from her purse and scrutinizing it. Then she seemed to come to her senses and her actions became urgent, she got dressed in a wild hurry, and left through the front door. There was some more security footage of her working her way downstairs and out of the building.

"We need to find her," announced Delman. "Correction," said Dexter. "You need to find her."

"Is that so." Marlow stepped back and considered what he had just seen, which looked to him like a person escaping captivity. "First you need to tell me why you had a woman imprisoned in that room. Under normal circumstances, that would be a crime."

"She wasn't imprisoned," said Matsumoto, spitting out the last word like she had just taken a bite of the most foul-tasting food imaginable. "She was there of her own free will, she had signed up for this procedure, and was being extremely well paid for it."

"You know that RainMan BioTech is involved in cranial implants?" Delman asked, his voice calm and measured.

Marlow nodded that he did indeed know about this.

"RainMan started working mainly with people that had severe spinal injuries, many years ago now. But as the technology and procedures advanced, they began operating on people with less debilitating injuries. During this phase it was discovered, quite by accident, that the implant technology could, as a side effect, cure addiction—all addictions."

Marlow's forehead rose in a question mark. "Seriously?"

Delman pointed at the screen. "That subject was an addict. Which her primary reason for undergoing this procedure."

He studied the woman on screen again. To his eyes she looked to be at peak fitness, well-toned, someone who worked out regularly. Not someone he would peg as an addict. In fact, there was something familiar about her—he knew this woman from somewhere, he just couldn't quite place it.

"Is there a secondary reason?" he asked.

Delman flicked a furtive glance at both Dexter and Dr. Matsumoto, as if they were discussing something telepathically.

"He might as well know the full story," said Dexter, waving a hand. "His nondisclosure agreement still applies."

"The subject has a state-of-the-art cranial AI implant," Delman continued. "It's based on our bio-chip technology and she can interact with the AI just by thinking about it. Not only that, she also has the ability to connect with any other AI within range of an RF signal—Wi-Fi, Bluetooth, that sort of thing."

"For real?" Marlow found this extremely hard to believe. These guys were bullshitting him.

"For real," Delman nodded.

He was stunned. Communicating with an AI by just thinking about it seemed like science fiction. But as Head of Security, he was just a little bit pissed off that they had not informed him of this research project going on in one of the executive apartments.

"Why wasn't I made aware of this? You come to me now after the horse has bolted?"

Again, there was that exchange of glances between the three, working out how much they were going to tell him. Eventually it was Dr. Matsumoto who spoke.

"Because this is a top-secret project, way above your pay grade."

"Oh really?" Marlow folded his arms. "Until you go and lose your prize racehorse."

"If you hadn't called for an evacuation then none of this would have happened," Dr. Matsumoto snapped back.

"Please." Dexter held up his hands. "What's done is done. We have a problem to solve and we won't solve it by acting like school-kids." He cast a stern glance at the doctor whose face looked like she was sucking a lemon.

"The truth is that there is a certain government security department with a three-letter acronym that is also involved," he continued.

"This is a military research project?" Marlow asked.

"In a way, yes." Dexter nodded. "They've been taking a hands-off approach so far. But if they find out we've lost our prize racehorse, as you put it, then... well, we all know what happened to Leon when StarLight was taken over."

"And you're worried that the same could happen here," said Marlow.

"Of course we are," snapped Delman. "We could lose control."

"Seems to me like you've already made a good start on that." Marlow leaned in closer to the screen where a full-body shot of the AI woman was freeze-framed. "So what was she doing in this building if this is a RainMan BioTech project?"

"After waking the first time, over in the research facility, she exhibited some, eh... side effects," Delman began to explain.

Marlow raised an eyebrow. "There always is, isn't there? Go on."

"She seemed confused, disoriented," Delman continued.

"Let's be honest, Harry," Dexter blurted in. "She was hysterical."

"Okay, yes, she freaked out," Delman admitted. "We believe

she may have temporarily lost her memory. She didn't seem to know who she was and what she was experiencing."

"That's one hell of a side effect," said Marlow.

"So we made the decision to sedate her and move her somewhere less clinical, somewhere more familiar, hoping that she would be calmer when she woke again. Hence the reason to bring her here to one of the executive suites." Delman nodded toward the next-door apartment.

"That was your inspired idea, Harry," said Matsumoto, whose face had now recovered from its lemon-sucking.

"And it worked," Delman snapped back. "Granted, probably a little too well. But your team was supposed to be monitoring her return to consciousness, yet you just let her come around without any medical supervision."

Dr. Matsumoto looked peeved and ready to defend her medical team, but Dexter intervened with a raised hand. "Drop it. This isn't going to help us now."

"So let me see if I have this all straight in my head," Marlow said, looking from one to the other. "You guys have been busy working on a top-secret military project to create a person with AI superpowers who's just escaped and is wandering around with no clue who she is or what she is—and you want me to find her?"

"Yes, well, I wouldn't quite put it that way, but that's the general gist of it," said Dexter.

Marlow pulled over an office chair and sat down, rested his arm on the monitor bench and looked at the frozen image on the screen. "Okay. Questions?" he said, getting down to business. "Firstly, I assume this... subject has a name."

"Dawn Harrison," Delman replied. "She was one of our employees, worked as a personal trainer in the gym."

A light went on in Marlow's head. "Of course, that's where I knew her from."

"You know her?" Delman asked, a little surprised. "She hasn't worked there for months, and even then, it was just part time."

Marlow looked up at Delman. "I had a few personal training sessions with her. She seemed pretty together, very athletic."

"She's actually an alcoholic, or at least she was," said Delman. "She gave it up two years ago after she was involved in a very nasty car crash. We'll get you the profile details. The reason she was chosen for this project is because she is officially an addict, so we have, eh... FDA cover for such radical treatment."

Marlow felt his phone vibrate in his pocket, fished it out, and saw that Delman—or more likely his AI—had sent him the profile. He took a moment to flick through it. "She's from around here, so probably has friends and family. Has she got any money?"

"There was around six hundred dollars cash in her purse, and a new bank card with a substantial sum deposited recently," said Dexter.

"How substantial?" Marlow asked.

"Half a million," replied Dr. Matsumoto.

"Wow. The price for having your skull opened up, I suppose?"

"That was the first half," Delman added. "The rest is due when she completes the training."

"Nice. Although, it looks like it wasn't really worth it." Marlow put the phone away and looked back at the three of them—all had an expectant look on their faces. "If what you're saying is true, and Ms. Harrison is wandering around in a confused state, then she's not going to get very far. We can start by thinking like her, working out where she might go, get some eyes on her home address and any family or friends she might have in the Bay Area. But I'm going to need some resources thrown at this. I'll need some people, specialists in finding missing persons."

Delman frowned. "Is that wise? We can't let this get out. Remember what happened to—"

"Yeah, yeah," Marlow cut him off. "Remember Leon. Look, they don't need to know anything about this." He waved a hand around at the medical equipment. "I just need boots on the ground with a mugshot in their hand. No one needs to know more than they have to."

"What about our own staff?" asked Dexter.

Marlow shook his head. "We're maxed out after the riot, we've got to do a full countersurveillance sweep of the building, as well as double up on all access points in case they try something again. We just don't have the people. Anyway, I know a few specialists in this area, people who know what they're doing, and don't ask any questions."

"Do it," said Delman. "Whatever it takes, just do it."

Marlow rose from his seat. "Okay then, I'll get right on it."

"Just one more thing," said Delman, as Marlow was leaving.

"Yeah, what?"

"Whatever you do, don't use a taser on her. The voltage could fry the chip in her brain."

"It's okay to shoot her, though," said Dr. Matsumoto. "Just not in the head."

Marlow nodded. "Okay, some useful health and safety tips. I'll keep them in mind."

# CHAPTER 9
# DROP EVERYTHING

J eb Marlow left the meeting with Harry Delman with a clear understanding that he had just dodged a bullet. The chaos of the riot had been a disaster, and if not for the disappearance of Dawn Harrison, he would be looking for a new job.

He remembered her. How could he forget? Around nine months ago, he woke up one morning and found himself on the wrong side of thirty-six and entering new territory on the scales. In a moment of self-reflection in front of the bathroom mirror, he decided it was time to go back to the gym and make some effort to halt the slide. That's where he met her, working as a personal trainer to the tech bros and sisters of the Neuromorph Corporation. To his eye, she was stunningly beautiful with the lithe muscular body of a dancer. He was smitten. It took him several weeks of visits to the gym before he finally booked a session with her. She was professional, quiet, competent. It took him another few weeks to work up the courage to ask her out on a date. But he never did.

Partly it was a work thing. He had dated colleagues before but it never worked out, and caused more trouble than it was worth. As soon as you started to get entangled with someone, the work atmosphere would subtly change. Some people would have their noses put out of joint, some that had fancied their own chances and now found themselves denied. But it worked both ways, some may have had a thing for him only to find he was now off the table. And then there were the conflicts of interest. It was a failed work romance that had finally pushed him to quit the Department and try his luck in the corporate world. But the real reason he didn't ask Dawn Harrison out on a date was because she left. One day she was there, working away in the gym, the next she was gone. He asked around but nobody seemed to know for sure what had happened to her. Some said she was on a long vacation, others said she just quit, and because she was a contractor and not a full employee, he had no file he could look up and find out. So, after a while, he just forgot about her.

Now here she was, a lab rat in one of Neuromorph's experiments. What had they done to her? How had she even agreed to this procedure? Yet, reading through the profile he'd just been given, he began to realize that beneath that elegant exterior, there lurked a very different woman. Maybe, that was another bullet he had dodged. Not that any of that mattered now. All he cared about was finding her and he knew just the guys for the job.

He took his cellphone out, found a quiet breakout space, and made the call.

"Tyler? It's Jeb. I got a job for you."

"Jeb Marlow, the man with the plan. What gives, after all this time?"

"Oh, same old, you know. Trying to keep the AI from taking my job."

"No escaping that path. It's the future, they say. So what you got?"

"Missing person. Your specialty. Easiest money you'll ever make. Here, I'm sending you the details." Jeb forwarded a greatly abbreviated file on Dawn Harrison.

There was a pause while Tyler scanned the details. "Nice, I can see why you'd want to find her. Say, wait a minute, this wouldn't be that trainer you had the hots for last year?"

He had to hand it to Tyler, he had an uncanny ability to retain even the most insignificant details. It was probably what made him so good at his job.

"Yeah, the same. But she's been involved in a Neuromorph project, may have suffered some memory loss, now she's gone wandering."

"Look Jeb, we'd love to help but we're up to our nasal hairs in tracking down the wayward offspring of the rich and famous."

"How much?" Jeb knew exactly what Tyler was after.

"Oh, I dunno. We'd have to drop a few cases for a while, lot of pissed off clients. Bad for the reputation."

"We'll double your usual rate. But you need to get on this

now. This should be easy, there's not too many places she can go," Marlow offered.

"Yeah, but then there's all the backlog we have to deal with after."

"Seriously, how much?" he asked again, becoming exasperated.

There was a momentary silence before Tyler came out with a figure. "Quadruple."

"Quadruple?" Marlow sighed. "Okay, okay, you got it. But start now. Drop everything else you're doing."

"Already on it. She'll be home before you know it."

# CHAPTER 10
# CIRCUIT MAGAZINE

A ssuming that the emaciated waif being hustled out of a courtroom a few years ago was indeed her, then that meant she had at least one other sibling. A brother. The image of him in the old photograph was in her mind as she made her way to a cheap hotel she'd found online. By the time she finally dumped her bag on the floor and sat on the lumpy hotel bed, it was late evening. The hotel was a collection of three two-story blocks organized around a parched courtyard with an empty pool. The room smelled of stale tobacco and sweat. The decor was a dull uniform beige. The furnishings were tired but functional.

She had planned to do some research on the Neuromorph Corporation, maybe gain some insight on what exactly they did. But the image of her brother kept coming back to her, so she googled him and headed down that rabbit hole instead. It turned out he was a technology journalist working for *Circuit*

*Magazine,* a leading online media company in the tech space, based here in the city. He had done well for himself, rising to the position of Executive Editor. She found plenty about him online, articles he had written, mugshots, and even a number of YouTube channels where he and a few others did tech reviews. Watching these videos, she struggled to drag anything up from the depths of her memory of Harrison family life. Nothing concrete came forward. Yet, there was something there, a connection of sorts. She couldn't quite capture it, but she could feel it.

Dawn considered how she might reach out to him. If she could make contact, and it turned out that he was indeed her brother, then he could help fill in some of the blanks, possibly even kickstart her memory. But how? Sending a simple email sounded like a good start. She probably had an account somewhere, but she currently had no knowledge of where it was or how to log in. Still, it would be easy to set one up on Gmail. And then what? Would he respond or think she was just some random female pretending to be his sister?

It was late, and Dawn began to feel the energy that had sustained her flight from Neuromorph beginning to drain away. She was tired and needed to get some rest. Maybe it was best to figure all this out in the morning. She lay down on the bed, rested her head on the lumpy pillow, and fell asleep.

~

Next morning, Dawn woke to bright sun filtering in through the slatted blinds, and for a brief moment, she was gripped with fear, fear that she was back in the medical facility in Neuromorph. But it quickly passed as she looked around the dull, shabby room and sniffed the stale smell. Yet, a new clarity had percolated in her mind overnight. Her brain had quietly worked through the many permutations of her situation and formulated a pragmatic solution for her to consider. To go back. To return to Neuromorph.

Dawn had to admit, given her current circumstances—low on money, no clue as to who she was, and few ideas on what to do next—it made a lot of sense. Maybe she overreacted to her situation. Perhaps there was a perfectly rational explanation as to why there was a widget implanted in her brain. And she was pretty sure they were looking for her anyway. How long could she realistically last out in the wild?

Yet, the image of her walking out of a courtroom, supported by her brother, was still etched in her mind. So she made a bold decision. With the little time and money she had left, she would travel to the headquarters of *Circuit Magazine*, where her brother supposedly worked, and see if she could find him— even if her chances of success were slim. If Neuromorph found her before then... well, so be it. Dawn gathered up her few belongings and, with a renewed sense of purpose, headed for the train station at Redwood City.

It took her forty minutes to get there, including stopping off for a cream cheese bagel and a coffee for breakfast. It was quiet at this time with only a few people waiting on the platform. As she approached the ticket machine, she began to feel that same tingling sensation in her head that she had experienced when she first woke up in Neuromorph. It was not painful, just very irritating. Yet it grew in intensity as she got closer. She did her best to ignore it as she tapped in her destination on the ticket machine, which presented her with the option to pay by cash or card.

*Maybe I should check if this bank card works?* she considered, even though it would probably put her name up in lights in some surveillance network somewhere. But since she had made up her mind to go back to Neuromorph, then what did it matter? The machine accepted the card and dutifully spat out a ticket. She had just put down a digital marker for anyone who might be trying to find her. *Let them come,* she thought.

Dawn took a seat on the upper deck of the train carriage. Not because of the views, but because they were single seats with fewer people around. An hour later, she hopped off again at the terminus at San Francisco Central. Less than ten minutes later, she was standing outside an old warehouse building in the South of Market neighborhood, the headquarters of *Circuit Magazine*. She entered.

While the exterior of the building might have been early twentieth-century industrial, the inside was full-on twenty-first-century techno-chic. All clean surfaces and minimalist design. Almost instantly, Dawn was assailed by an intense tingling sensation on the right side of her head. She instinctively cupped a hand over the side of her face, which seemed to lessen the feeling. It was happening a lot, this weird buzzing in her head; first when she woke up, then at the Starbucks, even the ticket machine for the train set off the same tingling as she got close to it. There was a pattern—the more electronic devices were around, the more her head buzzed. Now it felt like a hive of angry insects inside her skull.

She took a few deep breaths. After a moment, the intensity began to drop. It was still there, but manageable. She walked toward the reception.

"Hi, eh... I'm looking for my brother, Jake Harrison. I'm his sister, and I'm, eh... just passing through town. Thought I'd drop in and surprise him." She gave her best smile.

The immaculately coiffed receptionist looked at her as if she were a fly that had landed in her glass of Chardonnay.

Dawn pulled out her driver's license. "Here, my ID. I am actually his sister." Dawn slapped it down on the highly polished white marble counter.

"Oh, no, it's not that," the receptionist said, waving a hand at the ID. "It's that he seldom works from here, maybe once a month. But you'll get him at home today." She beamed.

The buzzing began amping up in Dawn's head; she was finding it difficult to focus. "Eh, do you happen to know where that is?" she gave an apologetic smile. "It's been a while since we spoke."

"I'm sorry but we can't give out that sort of information. Maybe just message him or give him a call."

The buzzing had reached an intensity where Dawn couldn't hide it anymore. She clapped a hand over the side of her head and screwed her face up with discomfort.

"Are you feeling okay?" The receptionist looked up at her with alarm.

Suddenly the buzzing stopped. *'Hello, can I help you?'*

It was a voice in her head, just like the one on the first day she woke up. "What the..."

"Are you alright?" the receptionist rose from her seat.

"No," Dawn waved a hand. "I mean yes, yes, I'm... fine. I just need to... sit down for a moment," she glanced over at a cluster of low seats, then back at the receptionist. "First trimester, you know how it is," Dawn lied, giving her best apologetic smile.

"Oh gosh, of course, please, let me help you." She rushed out from behind the marble block that was the reception desk.

*'My analysis of your bio-stats indicates that you are not in fact pregnant. My apologies if this causes you any distress.'*

Dawn put her hand on her forehead. "Stop, stop talking to me."

The receptionist froze.

"No, no not you, sorry, I'm just a bit..." Dawn gestured at the seats. "I'll just sit, I'll be fine in a moment, thank you."

"Eh, okay, sure. Can I get you anything, a glass of water?"

"No, no, I'm fine, really." Dawn backed away and sat down with her head in her hands.

"You're not going to be sick or anything?" the receptionist stepped back.

Dawn raised a hand. "No, all good. Just be a moment."

*What the hell is going on,* she thought as she tried to calm down.

*'You were inquiring as to the location of your brother, Jake Harrison,'* came the voice in her head again.

Dawn's instinct was to get up now and run out of here as fast as humanly possible. But she had done that once before and she wasn't so sure it had been a good idea. She took a few breaths and tried to calm herself down. Then, with the uncertainty of someone who isn't quite sure if they're losing their mind, she voiced a question in her head, carefully articulating with a conscious inner voice. *'Who are you?'*

*'I am Kurt,'* came the reply. *'The Circuit Media Corporation's general AI. I can assist you with a great many tasks. I'm here to help.'*

Dawn thought for a moment. Either A, she was actually losing her mind; or B, she was conversing with an AI by thought alone. Both options seemed equally crazy. Nevertheless, she decided to run with it.

*'How am I able to communicate with you?'*

*'Because you established a connection. So I am ready to assist.'*

*'A connection?'*

*'Yes.'*

Dawn considered asking it how this was at all possible, but since the receptionist was giving her ever more concerning looks, she figured she shouldn't hang around here too long.

*'Do you know where my brother, Jake Harrison, is right now?'*

*'Of course. Normally, this information would be restricted; however, since you have interfaced with admin privileges, I can inform you he is at home, playing Baldur's Gate 3, and has just died in the game by falling into a chasm on level five.'*

*'Do you have the address?'*

To her surprise, it gave her an address in Pacific Heights. Dawn reached into her bag, pulled out her new phone, and took a note of the address.

*'Thank you,'* she said.

*'My pleasure, I am here to assist. Is there anything else I can help you with?'*

'Don't suppose you can call me a taxi?' Dawn really just thought this as an aside, not meaning to actually ask the AI.

'Certainly, searching for available drivers now.'

'No, it's okay,' Dawn replied in panic. 'I can't really afford a taxi.'

'The fare will be on the Circuit Media account. You do not have to pay for it.'

'Well, okay then,' said Dawn.

'Done. A driver will be here in approximately thirty seconds.'

'Wow, that was quick.'

'He was just around the corner waiting for a fare.'

By now, the receptionist was whispering sweet nothings in the ear of a security guard and pointing over at Dawn. It was time to go.

She heard someone call her name.

"Dawn Harrison, taxi for Dawn Harrison."

She looked up to see the driver entering the lobby.

"That's me." She jumped up and started leaving, turning back to wave at the receptionist. "Thanks, much better now."

'Will that be all?' the AI's voice resonated in her head.

'Yes, thanks.'

'Terminating connection.' The tingling sensation in her head returned, but not quite as bad. It faded completely when Dawn finally left the building.

# CHAPTER 11

## YOU HAVE MY WORD

The taxi took Dawn north toward Pacific Heights, a very expensive neighborhood judging by the grand houses that lined the streets. It stopped outside an art-deco two-story house along Vallejo Street. Clearly, her brother, Jake, had done well for himself.

"That's on account, isn't it?" Dawn asked, just to be sure.

"Yup, *Circuit Magazine*. You have a nice day now."

She got out, and the taxi sped off leaving her standing on the sidewalk looking up at the imposing front door. Not quite sure of what to expect, she mounted the steps, rang the doorbell, and waited.

"Yeah?" an impatient male voice answered.

"Jake?"

"Yeah, what do you want?"

"Jake Harrison?"

"If it's a delivery, just put it in the box by the side of the porch."

"It's Dawn... your sister." She held her breath and waited.

"Dawn?"

"Yes, it's me."

"What the hell are you doing showing up here after all the crap you pulled?"

She was completely taken aback by this reaction, and since she had absolutely no memory of her past, she struggled to come up with a response. However, this was definitely the right place. There was a family past at work here, albeit a troubled one.

She gathered herself together. "I just need to talk to you."

"No way, not after the last time. I'm sick of your dramas. Go take it somewhere else." There was a click as the intercom went dead.

Dawn was stunned. Clearly they had some bad history and it sounded like she was the cause of it all. Yet she was at a loss as to how to respond. She assumed he could see her in the camera and wondered if she should drop her hoodie and show him her head, or would that just freak him out even more? She pressed the doorbell again.

It took a moment for him to answer again. "I told you before, I'm fed up being dragged into your crap. And now you show up after, what... two years?"

"Eh, I just need to talk to you for ten minutes, that's all. I promise I'll go then, just ten minutes." She reckoned he'd at least give her a few minutes, regardless of whatever had gone on between them.

"I'm not giving you any more money, if that's what you're looking for."

"No, no, I'm not looking for money or anything like that."

"Then what do you want?"

She wondered what she should say. Tell him about waking up in a research lab with a thing in her head? Tell him she had lost her memory? She suspected he wouldn't believe any of that. At least not right now, from out here on the porch.

"There's something... you need to see. But it's better I come in and show you. Ten minutes. Then I'll go. You have my word."

There was a long pause and Dawn wondered if he had hung up the intercom again.

"You'd better not be drunk."

"No, I'm not drunk."

Again, another long pause before the door clicked open. She stepped into a short hallway. At the far end, Jake was standing framed in an open doorway that led to a bright open living area beyond. He looked exactly like he did in the photo outside the courtroom. Tall, thin, same shaggy hair and beard. He was dressed in shorts and a t-shirt—work-from-home clothes.

"Ten minutes," he said, after giving her the once over. Then moved back inside to the living area. Dawn followed.

It was a bright cavernous space. At the far end, a row of glass doors opened out onto a Japanese-style Zen garden. On her right, was a huge sofa facing a gigantic screen set into a library wall full of books, games, and knick-knacks. On her left, was a kitchen that looked like it had been designed by NASA. There was consumer tech everywhere, scattered around on every surface—unsurprising, given Jake's profession as a tech journalist. She felt the tingling in her head start up again, but willed herself to ignore it.

Jake was standing on one side of the kitchen island, fiddling with a complex-looking coffee maker. He nodded at a high stool. "Grab a seat. Want a coffee?" His tone seemed to have mellowed a little.

"Sure." She sat on a stool, rested her elbows on the counter.

The machine hissed and spat and eventually he placed a tiny espresso cup in front of her. "Okay, you've got ten minutes to show me whatever it is that has you beating a path to my door after all this time."

Dawn studied her brother for a moment. There was definitely a familiarity there, the way he stood, the way he spoke, the way he set down the coffee cup. Past images flashed in her mind, connections to moments in their shared history. But it was all cloudy, hidden behind a veil. She wondered where to begin, how best to use the time, and how to gain his trust and get some answers.

"Do you know a corporation called Neuromorph?" she began.

"Yeah, of course." He said this like she had just asked him if he'd ever heard of Santa Claus. "Everyone knows Neuromorph. What about them?"

"Do you know what they do?"

He hesitated for a second, trying to figure out where this conversation was going. Or maybe he just didn't trust her. He sipped his espresso and leaned back against the kitchen counter. "AI bio-chips. They patented a revolutionary type of computer chip based on organic brain cell biology. Extremely radical, and potentially extremely profitable. Some say they're on track to be the most valuable corporation on the planet. Others say they're going to crash-land and all their scientists will burn in hell." He took another sip from his dainty little cup. "So what have they got to do with you?"

"Two days ago, I woke up in a hospital bed in one of their research labs, with absolutely no memory of how I got there or even who I am. My past is a complete blank." She gave a resigned, expansive gesture with her hands.

Jake raised a skeptical eyebrow at this admission.

"Worse," she continued, "there was an AI of some kind wired directly into my brain." She dropped the hoodie, took off the baseball cap, and tilted her shaved head so he could see the bandage.

"Woah!" His whole body jerked, almost dropping his dainty cup, coffee spilling over its edge. He recovered, then leaned forward a little, studying her head. "Holy cow, that's... that's... intense."

"So all that stuff you were saying about me over the door intercom—I have absolutely no memory of it. It's all a complete blank."

"So, you're saying..." he moved closer, never taking his eyes off her head, "that Neuromorph implanted some tech in your brain?"

Dawn nodded, "I think so."

Jake straightened up and gave her a skeptical look. "Wait a minute. If you've lost your memory, how come you knew to come here?"

"Google. I may have no memory of my past, but I still know how the world operates." She proceeded to give him a potted history of her escape from Neuromorph, searching the internet for clues as to who she was, and eventually tracking him down. She left out the conversation with the AI, Kurt. He might not be ready for that just yet.

When she'd finished, he let out a long, slow sigh. "That's quite a story," he said, shaking his head. "You know, of all the crazy stories you've come up with in the past, this one is on a whole new level. It's like, from another dimension." He did a head-exploding gesture with his hands.

"You think that's crazy, wait until I tell you the rest of it."

"Jeez, there's more? I think I'm going to need another coffee for that, maybe even a beer." He caught himself. "Eh, let's make that water." He opened the fridge and pulled out two small bottles.

Dawn reached into her bag and pulled out her purse. "I found this... prayer... among my things, you know the one they use in AA meetings." She slid it across the countertop. He passed her the bottle of water and picked up the small card, a curious look on his face.

"So, I'm guessing I was an alcoholic?" Dawn said this more as a question seeking an answer.

"Oh boy, and then some," her brother said, confirming her own fears. "You were the real party girl, always jetting off to some exotic location with your high-flying friends. That was until the... eh."

"The crash?" she prompted.

"Yeah," he nodded solemnly. "You were a complete mess

back then." He paused for a moment, studying her. "Do you remember the last time you were here?"

She gave an apologetic shake of her head. "Like I said, I have flashes, feelings, but nothing concrete. I do remember some images from the crash, but can't be sure they're actual memories."

"Well, it was just after the trial. You were here, drinking yourself into oblivion. It got to a point where we, eh... had a frank discussion about your life choices. You stormed out and, well... I haven't seen or heard from you until now."

"I sound like a complete mess. Maybe it's better if I don't remember."

"You were a minor celebrity for a while, famous for being a train wreck. You must have seen all the stuff about you on the internet."

"I didn't get that far. The first thing I found was all the stuff about the crash. I spent most of my time going down that rabbit hole."

Jake looked at his sister for a long, considered moment. "You know, Dawn, I'll be honest with you, apart from the enormous bandage and a shaved head, I've never seen you look so well. You look... healthy, toned, like an advert for a fitness center."

"The weird thing is, I don't feel like an alcoholic, but then again, I'm not sure I would know. Not that I'm going to tempt fate," she lifted the bottle. "I'll stick to the H2O."

She snapped the cap and took a swig. "But I haven't told you the crazy part of all this yet."

"You're kidding me? There's more?"

She jerked a thumb over at the big screen. "Tell me, were you playing Baldur's Gate 3 around a half hour ago? Did you die falling into a chasm on level five?"

Jake looked at her with equal parts astonishment and incredulity. "Eh, yeah. How did you know?"

"Kurt, the AI in your building, told me."

"What?" he jerked his head this way and that as if looking for a hidden camera.

"Wait." He snapped back to look at her. "That AI is for internal use. How the heck did you get access to it?"

"When I woke up that first time, before I freaked out, I heard this... voice in my head. It was the Neuromorph AI, Morph. Then, when I got out of the building, I started noticing this tingling sensation in my head anytime I was around a strong data signal." She looked around. "I'm getting it in here, with all this tech around. Anyway, it became extremely intense as soon as I entered the *Circuit Magazine* building, almost debilitating. Then, well, it just kind of stopped, and the AI started talking to me. In here." She tapped on the right side of her skull. "And the weird thing is, I could talk back. It was a two-way conversation just by simply thinking about it. It even booked me a taxi to get here, on *Circuit*'s tab."

Jake's face seemed to be drained of blood. "This is... incredible. It's a lot to take in." He leaned in and studied her head a little more. "You really think they put something in there?"

Dawn shrugged. "Yeah, a brain implant of some kind."

"Wow, this is... I don't know... seismic. If this is true then the world is about to shift on its axis." He began pacing around, gesticulating in the air as all the ramifications of this technology tumbled into his mind. "A mind–machine interface. So that's what they were doing. I knew they were up to something, we all knew, but this..." He looked back at Dawn again. "This is literally mind-blowing."

He stopped pacing, came around from behind the counter, and leaned in over her examining the bandage. "Have you taken this off? Do you know what's under it?"

Dawn raised a hand. "No way. Don't touch it. I don't want to know. I'd rather just get my memory back. The old me, warts and all."

"The old you was a disaster area, Dawn. But now..." he stood back to get a good look at her, "this new you looks great and even has superpowers."

"I've lost my memory, Jake," she reminded him. "And some evil corp has been screwing with my brain." She was getting emotional, she wanted to scream and shout and break something. But she didn't, maybe that was the old Dawn—it sure sounded like it. But she would not do that. She would calm herself down, get a grip, and figure this out.

"I don't have much time," she said eventually, almost to herself.

"No, it's okay." Jake jumped at her, holding out his hand. "I mean, forget what I said about the ten minutes."

She got a flash of a very old memory, of her brother picking her up after she fell off her skateboard. It was a long time ago, but it came into her mind as fresh as a new day.

"It's not that," she said, "it's just... I think they will be looking for me, Neuromorph. They'll want their experiment back. I'm actually surprised they haven't caught up with me yet."

"Yeah, I hadn't thought of that but you're right, they'll be searching for you." Jake scratched his chin, thinking.

"It doesn't matter. I've resigned myself to going back," Dawn continued.

"What? Are you serious?"

"Let's face it, they're the only people who really know what's going on," she said. "I mean, think about it. How did I end up in their research lab? From what I can figure, out I went willingly, so I must have known what I was getting myself into."

"We need to document this now, before they find you." Jake suddenly became a man of action, dashing over to a work desk and picking up his phone.

"What do you mean?"

"People need to know what they're doing over there," he said. "You saw the protests, didn't you?"

"Yeah, but..."

He gave her a serious look. "Listen, there are things you don't know. Around a year ago, Neuromorph acquired another company called RainMan BioTech, who were involved in developing cranial implants. Speculation was rife that Neuromorph were planning to develop a brain interface using their bio-chip. However, this would not get FDA approval without a serious amount of non-human testing—which involves serious money and would take years, if at all. But there have been rumors that they were doing it in secret. You're the proof of that. This is big, Dawn. You've no idea how big it is."

# CHAPTER 12
# OPTICAL INTERFACE SKULL

D awn knew that time was not on her side. Once she'd
bought that train ticket with her card, she was pretty
sure an alert was blinking on some cyber-sniffing system
somewhere. That transaction put her at a certain place at a
certain time, and no doubt there would be an AI calculating
where she would most likely be going next. Heck, they didn't
even need an AI to figure out where she was going. Soon,
Neuromorph would come calling.

She was not sure what she hoped to get from her brother,
Jake. Was she expecting all the memories to come flooding
back? For him to fill in all the blanks for her? He had his own
blanks too. Two years where he had no knowledge of what she
had been up to, not even if she were dead or alive. Now, he
seemed more fixated on the thing in her head than reminiscing
about their shared past.

Her head began tingling again. It had been there in the

background ever since she stepped into the house, but she had ignored it to a point where she had almost forgotten about it. Now it was ramping up, impossible to ignore. A small, elegant microdrone flew into the kitchen area and landed on the countertop, a few inches from her empty coffee cup. Its sensor pod with a prominent camera lens rotated in her direction. It was studying her.

*'Hi there. I'm Whizzy. I'm here to serve and protect,'* the voice resonated inside Dawn's head. Surprisingly, she didn't freak her out—she was becoming accustomed to this strange ability the implant gave her. She pointed at the little machine while looking over at Jake. "What's this thing?"

"Oh that. It's a prototype surveillance drone. Semiautonomous. We got several sent to us for a tech review but the company went out of business before we got a chance to do anything." Jake came over to the counter again, looking down at the drone. "It was designed for schools. It was supposed to fly around looking out for trouble. It has an inbuilt taser and could take action autonomously if it spotted someone about to do bad. Although, I can't imagine anything that small would have any effect other than a cattle prod. Needless to say, a lot of people had issues with allowing a weaponized drone anywhere near a schoolyard, not least the insurance people."

"And you just let it fly around your house?"

"Sure. It's kinda cool. It just does its own thing." He waved a hand around in the air.

"So I noticed." Dawn focused back on the little drone, forming a question in her mind.

*'So what can you do, Whizzy?'*

*'I'm here to serve and protect,'* it repeated.

*'Can you fly up and land on my brother's head?'*

*'Of course.'* With that, the little drone powered up its rotors, rose up in the air, and gently landed back down on a very surprised Jake. He stood still so as not to upset its balance. His eyes darted upward then over to Dawn. "Are you... controlling it?"

*'You can come back now, Whizzy,'* she instructed. The drone complied.

"Yeah." She glanced over at Jake who was patting his hair back down.

"That's incredible." He lifted up his phone and started recording. "Do that again. Make it do something else." He held the phone toward Dawn.

"I really don't think putting me on camera is a good idea, Jake. I'm in enough trouble as it is."

"No, this is important. You've no idea how big this is. It's going to change everything. The world's gotta know what Neuromorph have been up to."

Dawn stepped off the stool and raised a hand. "No way, I don't want to be recorded. You'd probably just stick it up on YouTube and that could be problematic if I go back."

Jake lowered the phone. "Okay," he said, his tone resigned. "But are you really serious about returning, after all this?" He gestured at her shaved and bandaged head.

"They're the only people who have the answers. I've no memory of how I ended up with this... implant. And let's face it, neither do you."

"That's hardly my fault..." he said, considering her the way a parent might an errant child, "since you chose to find your future in the bottom of a glass and shut off all contact."

"I've no memory of that." Dawn shrugged.

Jake shifted a little uneasily, "Sorry, that was a bit harsh, don't mind me. It's just—" He waved a hand around gesturing vaguely in her direction. "You show up after all this time and, well... now you're a cyborg."

Dawn reached up and touched the bandage at the side of her head as if to confirm Jake's observation. "That's why I need to go back. I don't want to be... a cyborg."

"Don't be so sure that Neuromorph will want that. The way they'll see you is as an extremely valuable piece of intellectual property, something that can make them an absolute fortune, and then some."

"Surely if I can do these things, there must be others with the same abilities," said Dawn.

Jake pursed his lips. "Maybe, but I wouldn't bank on it. You might be unique."

"Even so, I need to go back, it's the only way," she said. "I simply can't survive out in the wild."

"Sure you can, you've got me." Jake smiled and opened his hands in an expansive gesture.

"I'm not running, I'm sick of running away," she said, the frustration building.

"Did you ever consider that going back to Neuromorph is actually... running away?" Jake folded his arms and fixed her with a hard stare. "Think about it," he continued. "Going back would be you running away from living your own life, on your terms."

Dawn thought about this. She had to admit there was an element of truth in what her brother was saying. But it made no difference, her mind was made up.

"If you're dead set on doing this then at least give yourself some leverage over them," he offered.

"What do you mean?"

He took out his phone again and waved it at her. "Get it on video, as much as is possible. Then let them know it's out there waiting to go live if they start being... problematic."

Dawn wasn't so sure. What could she do on camera that couldn't be regarded as faked? Her shaved head and the bandage didn't prove anything. Even seeming to control the drone with her mind could easily be done through some simple trickery.

"I'm not sure," she said. "Most people will just see it as a fake."

"Probably," her brother admitted. "But plenty of people will see it as true, enough to possibly cause problems for Neuromorph. And in that case, it gives you some leverage over them."

Dawn mulled this over, all the while conscious of the fact there could be a knock on the door at any moment with a bunch of the corporation's goons ready to take her away. "Okay," she finally conceded. "Let's do it."

"Great." Jake's face lit up.

"But I have your word you're not going to stick this up on one of your YouTube channels?"

His face turned solemn as he slowly shook his head. "Absolutely. Not unless you instruct otherwise."

Over the next thirty minutes or so, Jake began working out an outline for the video as well as setting up a table beside a blank wall so that there would be nothing in the footage that could identify a location. Dawn, being hungry, began to raid her brother's fridge and make herself a sandwich. By the time she had finished, Jake had worked out a plan.

Dawn would sit at one end of the table, side-on to the camera, with the little drone resting on the table a short distance away. In front of her were a small stack of index cards lying face down. She would first shuffle them, read the instructions on the top card, and place it back to one side. Then she would focus her mind and instruct the drone to do whatever was written on the card. Lift off, shift right, land back, and so on. Jake would later add in text on the footage with these instructions. Dawn still reckoned it could all be faked, but when she watched it back an hour later, she had to agree it had an eerie, almost paranormal quality to it.

"We need to get some close-up video of your head," Jake announced, whipping out his phone again and zooming in on her bandage.

"Wait a minute, what's this?" With a free hand, he began tugging at a flap of bandage just behind her ear.

"Stop!" Dawn reached up to grab his hand. "Don't go pulling it off."

But he was now using the zoom on the phone to get a much closer look. "Woah!" He shifted back in surprise, then moved in again.

"What? What are you seeing?" A twinge of concern rippled through her body.

"Well, I'll be damned, but it looks to me like you have a tiny optical interface port grafted onto your skull, just behind your ear. Wow!"

He stopped recording, then replayed the video for her. Sure enough, she could see a tiny square port that was most definitely not a product of nature.

"What the hell is that?" Her hand reached up behind her ear. She could feel its hard, engineered edges.

"It's used for very high-speed data transfer. It's probably what you were plugged into before you woke up. This is mega. It goes a long way to proving your story, that Neuromorph has been messing with your head." Jake was almost dancing with excitement.

Dawn didn't share his excitement; in fact, quite the opposite. She felt drained and exhausted. The entire ordeal was beginning to catch up with her. Her brother must have picked up on this as he suggested she could go and have a rest while he worked on editing the video. She reluctantly agreed, not really wanting to stay the evening, but she was dead on her feet. Perhaps controlling the drone took more energy than she had realized.

"Come on, I'll show you where you can crash out for a while."

She followed him through the house to a guest room. Then he left her. Dawn lay down on the bed and was asleep in minutes.

# CHAPTER 13
# MANDY MAX

Malik Al-Sayf unrolled a well-used cleaning mat over a table on the balcony of his room within the sprawling Waleed bin Saeed family property nestled in the Hillsborough area of San Francisco Bay. Seventeen thousand square feet of palatial luxury set in four acres of mature, manicured gardens —just one of the many such properties owned by the family dotted around the globe in every major city that mattered. Strictly speaking, it was owned and managed by an investment company but was always available for any family members that should find themselves in this neck of the woods and needing a place to put their feet up. Mostly it was never used, yet was meticulously maintained by a staff of four, specifically for those few short weeks in the year when it might be needed.

From his vantage point on the balcony, Malik could look down over the swimming pool—its glassy water now reflecting a bright half moon—and across the verdant expanse of the estate's lush gardens. His long black hair was still wet from a late-night swim, tied back in a ponytail.

He sat down and proceeded to lay out two handguns on the mat, each a favorite in its own way, and each had its own strengths and shortcomings depending on the task required. Alongside them, he placed a Sparrow 22 silencer and well-used cleaning kit contained in a soft, aged leather pouch. Neither of the two handguns nor the silencer required cleaning, but that was not the point of this procedure. This was more of a ritual. Something he did to relax the mind and body. He began with the Ruger Mark IV Hunter, firstly removing the magazine, then checking to ensure that there was nothing loaded in the chamber. When he was satisfied that the gun was empty, he began to disassemble it.

As he worked, his mind began to reflect back on recent events. The riot he had orchestrated at the Neuromorph campus had been extremely effective. The HQ building had been successfully infiltrated and various discreet surveillance devices planted here and there. These would be found, of course. That was the point. It was sleight-of-hand, a deception to keep eyes off the real mission.

Prince Waleed bin Saeed, for his part, had no knowledge of this subterfuge. Yet, Malik did detect a hint of vanity. The prince had an overinflated sense of his own self-importance and thought that the protest was because of his scheduled visit. Nothing could be further from the truth, but it served Malik's purpose well—and those of his real paymasters.

In reality, once the tour of Neuromorph's most secure facility had been granted to the Saudi investment delegation, a carefully crafted industrial espionage plan began to unfold. It started with a barrage of social media misinformation flooding into the feeds of those deemed most affronted by the crimes against nature that were being perpetrated by the mad scientists in Neuromorph. A physical protest was called and a date was suggested. Ultimately, the bait was taken. It never failed to amaze Malik just how easy it was for his paymasters to manipulate that portion of the population that lived mostly on a diet of misinformation and outrage.

Malik then hired the necessary people to create enough chaos to break through the security cordon. Several of his own operatives were seeded into this "rent-a-mob" with a mission to plant the surveillance devices. All this had gone spectacularly well, but it was still just a diversion. It was hoped that all this chaos would focus Neuromorph's security resources on the protest and the subsequent cleanup operation. They would not be looking too closely at the Saudi delegation that were being given access to the most restricted areas in the entire Neuromorph campus—the bio-chip fab and datacenter.

Earlier that week, in a busy coffee shop down near Fisherman's Wharf, Malik had taken a seat at the counter beside a young Asian woman wearing a pink scarf. He ordered a black coffee, and while the barista busied himself preparing the brew, the young woman placed her cellphone down on the counter close to Malik. A few moments later, she left the cafe and Malik pocketed the cellphone.

It looked like any other high-end Android phone. Except this had a payload that could inject itself into any other nearby device using NFC (near field communications). What this payload did exactly, Malik was not sure, nor did he care. All that concerned him was that it was to be placed as close as possible to any of the cellphones used by the Neuromorph executive team. This had been accomplished at the investors' tour earlier that morning. Security protocols at the bio-chip fab required every person entering to be relieved of all personal electronic devices, which were then placed in a secure lock box to be retrieved later on exit. This was the opportunity for Malik's new cellphone to do its thing and infect all adjacent devices. Yet, there was much that could go wrong. The victim devices needed to still be powered up and have NFC active— neither of these states was a given. This meant that his true paymasters would not know for quite some time if the operation had been successful. Yet, considering that it had taken almost five months of planning to get to this stage, another few hours would make little difference. Still, he needed the ritual of cleaning to keep him distracted while he waited for confirmation that the mission had been a success—or a complete failure.

Malik finished reassembling the Mark IV Hunter, placed it carefully back down on the mat, then moved on to the FN Five-seveN. He had just removed the magazine when his phone pinged. He leaned over to read the alert on screen.

*Mandy Max. Call me. I show you good time.*

It was the alert he had been waiting for. A message from his handler to get in contact. He picked up the phone and hit callback. Almost instantly, an encrypted video connection was established. An AI-generated head and shoulders of a young

Asian woman materialized and began speaking in a slightly uncanny AI-generated voice.

"You'll be pleased to know that we are more than satisfied with the outcome of today's events."

Malik took this to mean that the cellphone hack went as planned.

"Subsequent analysis of these outcomes, along with the fortuitous occurrence of some additional third-party intel, has now presented us with a unique opportunity. One that we had not envisaged pre-mission. And one where we feel you are best placed to act on our interests."

Malik had assumed his role in the mission to infiltrate Neuromorph's communications security was now at an end. However, this sounded like they had other plans for him. He would not get out of this so easily.

"As suspected," the young AI-generated woman continued, "we now have confirmation that Neuromorph has been working on a brain-AI interface ever since their acquisition of RainMan BioTech. We believe this research has provided a significant breakthrough in the form of a human subject with an AI implant, that can also interact with any other AI using only thought."

Malik was stunned, so Waleed's suspicions were right all along. Yet, he guessed from the conversation that was happening right now, it would not be the Saudis that gained from this knowledge. They simply had no idea of how much they were being played.

"In a stroke of good fortune, we also believe that this subject executed a successful extraction from the Neuromorph compound during the riot. She is now roaming free, we presume somewhere in the greater San Francisco area. This has been somewhat corroborated by a short video uploaded to our TikTok social media platform earlier this evening."

The video clip began playing. A young woman, with a shaved and bandaged head, sat across the table from a small drone. A voiceover informed the viewer that "she is a subject in a top-secret program to develop AI mind control. More shocking revelations will be revealed in subsequent videos, so make sure to subscribe to the channel and hit the like button."

The woman shuffled a deck of index cards, placed them face down on the table, and selected the top card. The text of this card was displayed onscreen for the viewer. *'Move the drone above the table surface three feet.'* The woman placed the card back down, concentrated, and the drone rose into the air, hovering approximately three feet above the tabletop. The video continued in this vein for another few minutes before ending.

Malik shook his head in amazement. *Is she really controlling that drone with her mind?* he wondered.

He asked the obvious question. "How do you know this isn't a fake?"

"We don't. However, the physical characteristics match those of a woman seen leaving the Neuromorph compound around the time of the riot."

Several still images now flashed on the screen, clearly taken from a security camera feed. The woman's head and face were obscured by a baseball hat covered with a hoodie. Yet there was a distinct similarity between this person and the woman in the TikTok video.

"We've identified her as Dawn Harrison, an ex-employee of Neuromorph, a fitness trainer in their corporate gym. We have also identified the voice of the narrator in the video along with the source of the upload. This corresponds to a Jake Harrison, the subject's estranged brother, a tech journalist. As a consequence of this intel, she has become our top priority. Your new mission is to find her, keep her safe, and bring her to us at a drop-off point yet to be determined."

Malik considered this for a moment. "This would seriously compromise my cover with the prince and the Saudis."

"It would. But they are of no consequence to us anymore. Their usefulness has passed. All that matters now is the acquisition of this subject."

"This could put me in a dangerous position if I were to be exposed," he cautioned.

"We appreciate your concerns, so we are willing to make it worth your while."

A large bitcoin amount flashed on screen, and from Malik's quick mental calculation, it would amount to over five million US dollars. A truly exorbitant figure, well above his standard fee.

"Of course, we will provide new identities for countries of your choosing."

Malik didn't need any more convincing, and the Saudis were beginning to bore him anyway.

"Double it. Half now, half on completion," he said, pushing his luck. But he reckoned they were desperate to acquire this subject before Neuromorph found her, as he was sure they would, and they had no other assets available, otherwise why were they risking blowing his cover.

There was a silent response—presumably they were considering this audacious bid.

"Agreed," came the flat response. "But a quarter now, a similar amount when we have confirmation you have acquired the subject. Final amount on handover at a point yet to be determined."

"And new US and Japanese identities," Malik pushed further.

"This can also be done."

"Okay, so what have you got for me to work with? Any background on her?" he asked.

"A fortuitous outcome of your earlier mission enables us to access the cellphone of Jeb Marlow, Neuromorph's Head of Security. Through this, we have established that two outside security contractors have been assigned to track down the subject. We will send you all transcripts of Marlow's conversations pertaining to this mission."

"Am I to assume they haven't found her yet?" he probed.

"Not yet. However, we do know that she used a bank card at Redwood City train station to buy a train ticket to San Francisco Central. Marlow suspects that she may be attempting to contact her estranged brother. Which this TikTok video confirms. We believe she is in his house in Pacific Heights, or was there as recently as four hours ago."

Malik nodded, "That would be a good place to start."

"Bear in mind that what we require is physically inside the

subject's head. Under no circumstances are you to injure her in such a manner that might damage this implant. This warning also extends to the use of tasers or any other high-voltage weaponry."

"Understood."

"One last thing. Failure is not an option with this assignment. I trust you understand the implications before accepting the mission."

By this, Malik knew that they would probably assassinate him if he didn't return with the goods. But from what he had heard so far, it should be the easiest money he'd ever make. Not only that but it would enable him to disappear and begin a completely new life, something he had been contemplating for quite some time. This was his way out.

"I have never failed a mission so far and I don't intend to start now. Let's face it... Mandy... that's why you pay me the big bucks."

"We are all glad to hear that." The call terminated.

# CHAPTER 14
# TO SERVE AND PROTECT

D awn awoke to bright sunlight streaming through the window blinds and the smell of freshly ground coffee. She extracted an arm from beneath the duvet and rubbed the sleep from her face. She felt surprisingly refreshed; she must have slept for a very long time.

*'Good morning, I trust you slept well,* came a voice in her head.

She lifted her head from the pillow in search of the source of this interloper. Perched on a side table was the little surveillance drone.

*'Is that you?'* she asked in her mind, giving it a stern look.

*'Yes, my apologies if I startled you. But it is very pleasant to have someone to talk to in the morning, don't you think?'*

*'Eh... yeah, well that would depend on the someone.'*

There was a knock on the bedroom door. "Incoming."

This triggered a long-forgotten memory. Her brother always said this when he was entering her room, an early warning.

"Yeah, I'm awake."

The door opened and he swooped in carrying a mug of hot coffee and a plate piled with pancakes. "Breakfast, I imagine you must be starving."

She accepted the coffee with outstretched hands. The pancakes, he placed on the bedside locker.

"How long have I slept?" she asked as the first sip of the day began to clear the fog of sleep from her body.

"Fourteen hours. You must have been exhausted." He then spotted the drone. "Ah, there you are. I was wondering where it had gotten to."

"Me and Whizzy have been having a wakeup chat." Dawn nodded over at it.

"I think it likes you." Jake smiled.

"It's a machine, it doesn't have... feelings."

"Oh, I'm not so sure." Jake sounded serious. "With some of these latest generation AI models, they can exhibit an uncanny affinity for certain interactions. Meaning that they seem to communicate better with some people more than others."

"That's weird." Dawn cast a suspicious glance at the drone.

Jake's phone pinged. He fished it out of his pocket and looked at the screen. "Uh-oh."

"What?"

He showed her the image on the phone screen. "That's the door intercom. And those two guys don't look like they're delivering pizza."

Dawn gently took the phone and studied the two men, both in suits, casual but smart. She handed it back to her brother. "Neuromorph?"

"Possibly. They must have tracked you down. But don't worry, there is another exit out the back. Quick, get dressed and I'll show you."

"Answer it, see if they are actually from Neuromorph."

Jake returned a look of horror. "Seriously? But..."

"But nothing." Dawn cut him off. "I decided I'll go back anyway. So if they are from Neuromorph, then maybe they can give me a ride."

Jake hesitated, no doubt thinking of a way in which to dissuade her from this course of action.

"I've made my mind up," said Dawn stiffly.

He sighed, lifted the phone up, and tapped the answer icon. "Yeah?"

"Hi," came the cheery response over the phone's speaker. "We're hoping you may be able to help us. We're looking for your sister, Dawn Harrison?"

"Oh yeah, and who are you?" Jake didn't hide his disdain.

"We're from Neuromorph. She was involved with one of our projects and we believe she may be in danger. We're trying to find her so we can help her."

Dawn grabbed the phone and held her face to the camera. "I'm here, and I've no problem going back. But how do I know you guys are who you say you are?"

Their body language visibly changed. They seemed relieved that they had found her but a little confused as to how they might verify their intentions. They had a quiet conversation with each other for a moment. Then seemed to come to some agreement. One started to make a phone call, the other went back to the intercom.

"We're making a call to our boss, who will get Harry Delman, the CEO, to call you. We believe your brother should be able to verify that it is actually him. Is this satisfactory?"

Jake's eyes widened. "Delman! Wow, they're bringing out the big guns."

"Do you know him?" asked Dawn.

"Sort of. I interviewed him once if that counts."

"Yes, that's acceptable," she replied back into the phone.

They waited. A moment later, the guy on the cellphone gave the thumbs up, and Jake's phone rang. He sat on the edge of the bed beside Dawn, held the cellphone up so she could see, and hit *accept*. On screen, she could see a very animated Harry Delman standing in a sleek office with a number of others beside him. Dawn thought she recognized the doctor from that first day that she woke up in the lab.

"Miss Harrison, we're so glad you're okay, we've all been very worried about you. We understand you're a little confused and overwhelmed by everything, but please be assured we are here to help you through this. We will do absolutely everything we can for you, but you must let us bring you back in where you can be more comfortable and have all your questions answered."

Dawn hit the mute button, and turned to her brother. "Is that him?"

"Yeah, that's him. Looks like they gathered a few people so that it's less likely to be an AI fake."

Dawn pointed at one of the people on screen. "I recognize her as one of the doctors from that first day."

She unmuted the mic. "Alright. Get my room ready, and I have a whole bunch of questions for you guys."

"Excellent, this is the right choice you're making. The two gentlemen outside your door are ready to escort you back. We'll see you soon."

"Okay," Dawn replied as she ended the call. She took a long sigh. "I suppose I better get packing."

*'Are you leaving?'* It was the drone in her head again, sounding crestfallen that she was deserting it.

*'Sorry, I have to go,'* she replied in her mind, feeling like she was abandoning a small child.

Jake stood up and headed for the door. "When you're ready, I'll meet you downstairs and we can open the door to these guys." He didn't sound happy about the prospect. "I'll be sorry to see you leave. I'm beginning to like the new Dawn. Much nicer than the old one."

"You sound like Whizzy."

"What?"

"The drone." Dawn jerked a thumb in its direction. "It's telling me it's sad to see me go."

"Seriously?" Jake's eyes widened.

"Yup."

"Then keep it," he said. "Take it with you. It can be your... er, friend."

*'Oh, please, please. I will do my very best to serve and protect,'* the drone's voice in her head pleaded.

*Why not?* she thought. It could be fun to have it around, maybe even useful. "Are you sure you don't need it, Jake? Like for a review or something?"

Her brother waved a hand. "No, I've got another two. And as I said, the company that made them went out of business a while back, so I won't be doing any tech reviews. But just promise me you won't try to taser anyone with it."

"I'll try." She smiled.

*'This is an excellent outcome. One which gives me great joy and purpose,'* said the drone.

*'Okay, just don't make me regret this,'* Dawn replied.

Around twenty minutes later, she was fully dressed—with the little drone packed up in her bag—and standing inside the front door of the house.

"Ready?" Jake asked.

She nodded. He opened the door and Dawn walked outside.

The two Neuromorph guys stepped aside. One gestured to a car. "This way."

The other wanted to carry her bag for her but she hung on to it. Finally, she turned back to her brother. "Thanks. For everything."

"Ah, that's what family's for. Just don't leave it so long the next time." He reached out and gathered her into a big embrace. "Call me, let me know you're okay."

They pulled apart. "Will do."

She turned around and headed for the waiting car.

# CHAPTER 15
# CHANGE OF PLAN

From where he had parked his van on the street, Malik Al-Sayf had a good view of Jake Harrison's front door. He was not too close and alongside some tree cover. He sipped on a black spiced coffee as he waited and watched. Beside him on the passenger seat was an open laptop, and an animated background floated across the screen. Music by Tariq Abdul-Hakeem warbled through the van's speakers and Malik sang along, biding his time on this fine San Francisco morning.

Now that the cellphone of Jeb Marlow had been hacked, he had access to all his data including voice calls. From this, he had learned that two outside security contractors would be showing up at this very spot anytime now. Sure enough, a car pulled up outside the house and two smartly dressed men stepped out. Malik flicked off the music, sat up, and paid attention. They walked up to the door and pressed the buzzer. Malik raised an eyeglass to get a better look. The optical unit also had a rifle mic attached. He pushed an earbud into one ear and listened. He caught snatches of words.

"She's inside... yeah... but being cautious... needs to be convinced... get on to Marlow... see what he says."

Malik put away the eyeglass and mic and reached over to the laptop and tapped an icon to run some bespoke Chinese agency spyware. This would allow him to listen in on the cellphone conversation with Neuromorph's Head of Security. Marlow pretty much entered panic mode and went off to find the CEO guy, Delman. Malik put away the laptop and waited as this scenario played itself out. It was clear that the woman was inside. She just needed to be convinced that these guys were the real deal. Soon enough, he sat up again as he saw the woman exit the front door, get into the car with the two guys, and head off.

He didn't follow. Instead, he closed the windows and returned his attention to the laptop. He lifted it off the passenger seat, placed it on his knees, checked his earbuds, and hit dial. *This had better work,* he thought, as he waited for the connection.

In the car that was taking the woman back to the Neuromorph compound, the security guy's cellphone rang. He answered. "Jeb, we're heading back. All good here, if that's what you're calling about."

This was the moment for Malik to find out if all this Chinese AI trickery he had installed in his laptop would actually work. They had convinced him that it was a state-of-the-art, real-time voice emulation. But he still harbored doubts, and no amount of trickery would be a substitute for simple persuasion. He needed to choose his next words very carefully.

"Change of plan," he said. "Delman wants internal security to take over."

What the security guy on the other end should be hearing was the voice of his boss, Jeb Marlow, calling from his cellphone. At least that's what Malik hoped he heard. There was an anxious moment while he waited for the response.

"Change of plan? Seriously?"

"Don't worry, you're still getting paid. The top dogs here are just paranoid, is all. Anyway, you're to hand over to internal at this location." Malik sent a set of coordinates.

"That's a parking garage. Are you sure that's right? Seems off the beaten track to me."

"Look, it's quiet, and protected," Malik explained. "No eyes looking down on us. Like I said, the paranoia levels are sky high here at the moment."

Again, there was a few seconds' delay and Malik could hear a discussion going on in the background with the other security guy.

"Okay, you're the boss. We should be there in fifteen minutes."

"Just make sure you are." Malik ended the call.

His heart was thumping, and with no AC blower on, his shirt was saturated with sweat. Shooting someone in the head was a lot less stressful than all this high-tech bullshit, he concluded. But it had worked. They had taken the bait.

He put away the laptop and started up the van. Then he dialed the coordinates into the GPS, and pulled out into traffic.

# CHAPTER 16
# SERIOUS HARM

Dawn made herself comfortable in the front passenger seat of the car as it moved off down Vallejo Street. "You guys got names?" she asked.

The driver, the older of the two by maybe a decade, jerked a thumb at himself, "Tyler, and baby-face back there is Ethan."

"So how'd you find me?" Dawn pretty much knew the answer, but she was anxious about her decision to return and tried to make conversation to lessen her unease. The GPS showed a journey time of thirty-two minutes back to the Neuromorph campus, so she was stuck with these guys for a while.

"Oh, it wasn't that hard. If you don't want to be found then don't use a bank card," said Ethan from the back.

"Or a phone," Tyler added. "Everything leaves a footprint these days." He said this like he was reminiscing about an earlier, simpler time.

Ethan's cellphone rang and he answered it, putting it up to his ear so only he could hear the conversation. It sounded like it was from his boss as he responded by giving an update.

"Change of plan," he said, pocketing the cellphone. "We're heading for a different handover point. They want internal to take over."

"Yeah, I got the gist of it," said Tyler. "We're still getting fully paid, right?"

"Too damn right." He then proceeded to give a set of coordinates which Tyler tapped into the GPS. "That's... a parking garage," he said, sounding a little surprised.

"Yeah, I know." Ethan pointed at the roof. "They're paranoid about eyes in the sky apparently."

Dawn picked up on the mood change. "Is this... a problem?"

"Nah, they just want you back in one piece," Ethan assured her. "You're hot property, you know."

"They're probably planning the old switcheroo," Tyler explained. "Three cars go in, but if you're being tracked from the sky then they won't know which one you're in when they all leave again."

"Who's watching?" asked Dawn, leaning forward and gazing up through the windshield.

Tyler looked at her as if she were just about the dumbest person he'd ever met. "You really don't have a clue, do you?"

"Chinese is my guess," said Ethan.

"Chinese?" This was news to Dawn. Then again, maybe these guys were just jerking her around, she couldn't really tell.

"Hey, it's cool. Relax, don't worry about it. Standard procedure." Tyler waved a hand in the air.

Yet Dawn felt the vibe in the car change. She couldn't quite put her finger on it, but these two guys seemed a little less at ease. Maybe there was some history between them and Neuromorph, but she had no way of knowing.

The parking garage had been attached to a shopping mall that was now all shuttered up and ready for redevelopment. The garage remained open, but with nothing to bring people in, it was quiet and mostly empty. They drove up to one of the upper levels, with fewer and fewer vehicles on each level as they ascended. Finally, they came out on the penultimate level. The place was deserted except for one solitary black van. Tyler brought the car to a slow stop some distance from it, rolled down his side window, and studied it for a beat.

"What do you think?" Ethan poked his head in between the front seats.

"Check with Marlow," he replied, not taking his eyes off the van.

Ethan hit call on his cellphone and put it up to his ear. It took a moment but eventually he got a satisfactory response. "All good, apparently," he said, pocketing the phone again.

"Hmmm... okay, but let's not be stupid about this." Tyler slowly drove over toward the parked van and came to a halt around ten yards away.

"You stay here," he said, placing a hand on Dawn's arm. "We'll go check it out."

They both got out of the car and Dawn could see they were keeping one hand on weapons concealed inside their jackets.

This did not fill her with confidence, so she reached down for the backpack that she had left in the footwell, hoping to activate the little drone. It was probably a useless weapon but at least it made her feel slightly less vulnerable.

A man stepped out from behind the back of the van, and he waved and smiled as he approached. "Hey, you made it. Is she here?" He nodded over at the car.

"Yep, safe and sound. And who are you?" said Tyler, sounding cautious.

Dawn heard two soft cracks in quick succession. She looked up in horror as Tyler's head snapped back, a spray of blood curling in the air. He collapsed against the hood of the car and rolled to the ground. Ethan whipped out his weapon, but not fast enough. Two more cracks—he jerked, then crumpled like a rag doll.

The sheer violence of the moment froze Dawn to the seat. The next thing she knew, the man yanked open the door, grabbed her by the arm, and dragged her out. She struggled, trying to break free until he put the muzzle of the weapon up under her chin. "Stop, or I'll do you serious harm."

Dawn stopped.

"They said not to shoot you in the head," he grinned. "But I can still put a bullet in you somewhere else." With that he dragged her to the back of the open van and pushed her in. "Face down, face down," he said, pointing the gun at her.

She complied. As Dawn lay on her stomach, she felt the pinch of zip-ties around her wrists and ankles. Then she was forced to sit up again, her back against the side of the van wall, while duct tape was wrapped around her mouth. Her heart raced, her mind a blank, consumed by the feeling of extreme fear. The rear doors slammed shut and a few seconds later, the van was heading out of the car park, carrying her to some unknown fate.

———

# CHAPTER 17
# SERVE AND PROTECT

Dawn's backpack, still nestled in the footwell of the now abandoned car, came to life as the small drone inside jiggled its way to freedom. It tumbled out onto the floor, tested its rotors, and flew up onto the dashboard shelf—just as a black van raced down the exit ramp. The drone immediately tried to communicate with Dawn, but received no response. The passenger door was wide open. The drone flew out, rose up in the air, and scanned its surroundings.

Two bodies lay on the cold concrete floor of the car park in a slowly expanding pool of their own blood, oozing out from exit wounds consistent with having been shot at close range. The drone ascertained that neither of the victims was Dawn Harrison. Yet, there was no sign of her. It tried to communicate again—still no response.

Within the timeframe of a few nanoseconds, it had analyzed

the entire scene and concluded that bad things had happened here, and that its ability to serve and protect had been severely undermined. The only course of action open to it now was to find Miss Harrison and ensure her safety... any way it could.

It calculated that there was a very high probability that she was in the van that it had tagged leaving this level. However, it could not rule out that she could be elsewhere in the car park, so it powered up its rotors and flew off to conduct a thorough search.

After scanning all other levels without finding her, it concluded that she must be in the van. However, it had lost valuable time. It exited the car park at maximum speed, rose high up into the sky, and began searching the surrounding road network looking for a pattern match for the van. After around half a minute, and several false positives, it categorically identified the van in a line of traffic waiting for a signal change. It dived down toward it, hoping to catch it before it moved off. It was fast, but would drain power quickly if it had to chase down a high-speed vehicle. Nevertheless, it must do what it was programmed to do. It angled its flight and dialed everything up to eleven.

But the signal changed and the van moved off before the drone had time to reach it. It decided to change tactics. Instead of burning through its energy store by chasing after it, it rose higher into the air to give it a much broader circle of vision. That way it could still keep track of the vehicle and conserve power. It had the advantage of straight-line flight while the van needed to follow the road layout.

After around twelve minutes, the van pulled off the road and into a gas station. The drone dropped down and landed on its roof. It tried again to communicate with Dawn.

'*Miss Harrison? Please respond.*'

# CHAPTER 18
# DRONE ATTACK

Dawn was flung this way and that as the van screeched its way down each level of the parking garage, all the while trying to wrestle free of the zip ties that pinched her wrists and ankles. But try as she might, she could not break them. By the time the van finally exited the parking garage and turned out onto the main road, Dawn was already battered and bruised from being slammed against the side walls multiple times. She lay face down on the floor, sweating and exhausted.

Now that they were on the main road, the van became more stable, the driving less frenetic and urgent. She managed to sit up with her back against the wall and take stock of her situation. She focused on calming herself down, slowing her heart rate, getting her breathing under control... and trying to think. What could she do, tied up as she was? Did she manage to activate the drone in time?

She voiced a thought. *'Whizzy, are you there?'* No answer.

From where she was sitting, she could see the back of her abductor. He had one hand on the steering wheel and a cellphone in the other. *Who the heck is this guy?* she wondered. *And what does he want with me?* But she kinda knew the answer. She was now a valuable piece of technology that a lot of people wanted to get their hands on. Yet she had never considered just how far they might go. This guy had brutally murdered two people just to grab her. She could still see the arc of blood flying off Tyler's head in her mind's eye. She shivered just thinking about it. This was a bad place she now found herself in—real bad.

Dawn watched as he tapped the screen of his cellphone and brought it up to his ear. He only talked in monosyllables, in a language she couldn't place. At the same moment, her head started tingling again. A sensation she was becoming familiar with any time she was around a data source.

*Not now,* she thought, shaking her head. *This was not what I need, yet another thing to contend with.* She struggled with the zip ties again, but it was not going to happen. Eventually, after the fourth attempt, she gave up. The buzzing in her brain was distracting her. She wanted rid of it, rid of this damn thing in her head.

Yet as she sat there, bumping along tied up in the back of a van, and running out of options, Dawn decided to turn her mind and focus on this incessant buzzing. This same sensation had occurred anytime she interacted with an AI. Like with the little drone or at Jake's office building, even that first day when she woke up in the lab. And if there was an AI around, then maybe she could connect, send a message or something. It was worth a shot since she had no other options.

As she focused, the frequency of the buzzing subtly changed and she discovered that she had some control over it, pushing it into the background or even amplifying it. When she did this, she was also able to discern that there was more than one signal. There were several overlapping, some very faint, almost background noise, others more prominent. Suddenly, the structure of the buzzing changed and Dawn realized that her abductor had just finished the call he was on.

*So that was one signal,* she thought. *But where are these others coming from?*

Dawn sifted through the remaining signals in her mind. Maybe the van had a rudimentary AI controlling the vehicle systems. Maybe she could talk to it?

'Hello?' she tried. No response. Yet, there was something. Not a clear voice response but a change in tone, a flash of something in her mind's eye. She tried again. *'Hello? Are you an AI?'*

Again no voice response, but there was definitely something going on, yet what it was and how to interact with it, Dawn had no idea. She tried again, but this time with no vocalization, she simply focused on the frequency. A series of fuzzy visual images flashed in her mind. She let out a yelp of surprise, fortunately muffled by the duct tape sealing her mouth closed.

*What the heck was that?* she wondered.

She tried again, focusing in on the signal and began to visualize what looked to her like a laptop screen, or possibly a tablet, or maybe it was the van's own media screen. Yet it lacked clarity. It was hard for her to get anything meaningful other than flashes of indistinct patterns.

The van took a hard turn and Dawn went flying across the floor again. By the time she righted herself, it had come to a stop. The guy got out and Dawn assumed that the back doors would be flung open and she would be dragged out into God knows what. But they didn't. Instead, she heard the *clunk clunk* of the gas tank being filled. She sank back and tried to get herself more comfortable; this could be a long journey.

*'Miss Harrison? Please respond.'*

Dawn sat up. Did she really hear that or was she imagining it?

*'Hello?'* she tried.

*'Oh, I'm so happy I found you. It's been quite a task to catch up with this vehicle.'*

*'Whizzy, is that you?'*

*'Yes, it is. I'm here to serve and protect.'*

*'Am I glad to hear your voice... in my head. Can you get me out of here? Can you call for help, send a message?'*

*'Unfortunately, my options are limited. I do not detect a Wi-Fi network that I can utilize that is within range. But I can return to an area where I can access a public network and send a message, giving your last known coordinates and the vehicle's plate number.'*

Dawn thought about this for a moment. It was better than nothing, but how long would it take for help to arrive? This guy could change vehicles at some point and if so, they would lose her again; she'd be back to square one.

*'Do you still have a working taser, Whizzy?'*

*'I do. However, I must advise that I have consumed a*

considerable amount of power in chasing down this vehicle, therefore my weapon system might not operate at optimal performance,' it cautioned.

'I'm pretty sure I can manage to get out of this van and get some attention if he can be disabled,' said Dawn, as she began to move herself into a better position.

'I can also assist in calling attention to your current predicament,' said the little drone.

'What's he doing now?' she asked.

'Filling the gas tank.'

'Okay, give me a moment to sort myself out here, then zap him. Taser that bastard.'

'Standing by.'

Dawn maneuvered herself onto her knees and shuffled up toward the open cab, then poked her head out from between the seats. Using the wing mirror, she could see the guy standing by the side of the van waiting for the tank to fill.

'Okay, Whizzy, do it!'

In the mirror, Dawn could just see the little drone fly into view overhead. The guy noticed it too as he looked up, startled. Two metal prongs spat out of the drone and embedded themselves in his chest, trailing a pair of thin metal wires back to the drone. The guy shook and yelled for a second or two, but still seemed to be able to move. He didn't drop to the ground like Dawn had hoped. Instead, he braced himself against the side of the van, reached up, grabbed the wires, and yanked the prongs out.

"Oh crap." Dawn realized this was not going to plan.

The guy then began pulling in the wires, dragging the

drone down, reeling it in. Finally, he grabbed it in his hand and smashed it against the side of the van.

By now, several other people at the gas station had looked over to see what the commotion was. The guy waved a hand, "All good. Just some crazy runaway drone."

Dawn froze. She couldn't scream for attention because of the tape over her mouth. But she could get herself into the driver's compartment and start a fuss. Maybe that would work, but it would not be easy; she needed more time.

*'Whizzy?'* Dawn called out in her mind, hoping against hope that the little drone had somehow survived. But there was no reply. She looked in the side mirror again to see the guy had stopped filling the tank and was moving back toward the van door.

*Damnit.* Her plan was turning into a disaster. She should have listened to the drone's advice and let it call for help. Now it was gone and she was still trapped. She couldn't move herself into the front seat in time to raise a ruckus. She had no other option but to lie back down on the van floor and pretend that she knew nothing.

# CHAPTER 19
# PLAN B

From the moment that Harry Delman learned that Subject 19 had vanished from the Neuromorph compound, his biometrics were all over the place. He had been micromanaging his stress levels ever since, trying to keep them within a tolerable range, just enough so that he could function. He had modified his nutrient intake to one optimized for mind–body harmony, which mainly involved copious quantities of Cannabidiol, otherwise known as CBD oil. His AI was working double time just keeping track of it all.

But Dawn Harrison had finally been located, staying over in her brother's house, and was now in the process of being driven back to the compound—willingly. He could feel the stress drain away from him as he sat cross-legged in his office, twelve minutes into his afternoon meditation session. He had brought himself to a point of profound stillness, of inner peace. A point in the session where he could now begin to focus on the true path, free from extraneous clutter and distraction. He dug deep, seeking enlightenment.

It came in the form of Dexter, bursting into his office. "Harry, wake up. I've just gotten a call."

This jarring intrusion exploded into Harry's blissful state, shattering his mind–body equilibrium and wrenching him back to reality, like a newborn being pulled screaming from the womb.

"Goddamn it, Gordon. How many times do I have to tell you to *never* interrupt my meditation sessions." He rose from the floor and stood up.

Dexter went to a sideboard and poured himself a stiff one. "This is important."

"Not as important as my meditations, they take priority over everything else. Please respect that."

Dexter snapped around and looked at Delman like an angry teacher. He clicked his fingers at him several times. "Hey, Earth to Harry, time to stop dicking around with inter-dimensional mind travels and come back to the real world where shit actually matters."

Delman stood silent for a moment while his personal AI read the room for him. "It is clear that your colleague has some critically important information to relay to you. His attitude is not a reflection on your personal recreational choices, merely a reaction to the news he is about to impart."

Delman sighed, "Okay, so what's going on? Has the subject arrived back yet?"

Dexter stood by the window, looking out. "I just got a call from our government overlords giving us a heads-up."

"What? Those vultures. What do they want now?" Delman asked.

Dexter took a sip from his drink. "To answer your first question. No, the subject, as you call her, has not arrived back. As to the second question, in a few moments, several government agents will be arriving here to start asking questions as to why two outside security guys, working on contract to Neuromorph, were found dead in an out-of-the-way parking garage." He turned to face Delman.

"Dead?" Delman couldn't believe what he was hearing.

"Shot in the head, twice, at close range. A professional hit job—so I've been informed. Needless to say, Dawn Harrison is nowhere to be found. And our government overlords are about to push the big red panic button."

"Oh crap." Delman felt as if he had just been punched in the stomach. He felt dizzy, he needed to sit down.

Dexter raised his glass. "Now you know why I needed a stiff drink."

"This is just the opportunity those parasites were waiting for, an excuse to come in and take over. They've no respect for the free market, for innovation. It's just... communism."

Dexter gave a long sigh, "It's not communism, Harry. It's called national security." He looked over and appraised his business partner. "Harry, you're a goddamn genius, one in a million. No... one in a hundred million. You've had the vision, and the drive, and the wherewithal to build one of the most valuable corporations in history. But it never ceases to amaze me just how little you actually know about the real world. None of this would have happened without the billions we received in government contracts. And we sure as hell wouldn't be researching cognitive augmentation without the legal cover they've been giving us."

Delman rose from his seat, walked over to the sideboard, and also poured himself a stiff one. "Screw it," he said as he downed it in one gulp. His AI vehemently objected to this intrusion of poison into his pristine body, it would seriously upset his carefully curated nutritional regime. Delman ignored it, snatched the AI glasses off his face, and threw them on the counter.

"This is just the first step, isn't it? The takeover begins. I'm going to end up like Leon after StarLight."

"You're being melodramatic, Harry. You need to look at it from their perspective. We lost our test subject, arguably the most valuable individual on the planet. And what's inside her head could be a very serious security threat to this country. Very sloppy."

"So what!" Delman spat back. "We can always make another one."

"Jeez, Harry. You don't get it, do you? She's been kidnapped, abducted, call it what you like, presumably by someone whose intentions toward this country are anything but benign. They have stolen our most critically important intellectual property. If they reverse engineer what's inside her head... then there goes the neighborhood. It *will* be used against us. And I don't mean Neuromorph. I mean the entire Western world."

"Now you're the one being melodramatic, Gordon."

"She has to be found, Harry. They can't let her fall into the wrong hands. Do you understand?"

Delman sat down again. The alcohol was beginning to take effect and he was feeling a little dizzy. "So how much do they know... about the breakthrough... about her potential."

Dexter shook his head. "I had to tell them, no keeping secrets now. Not from these guys."

"Goddamnit. What a mess."

"I only gave them the highlights. They're going to be here soon and they'll be looking for answers. We've got no option but to play ball as they're the only people who have any chance of finding her now."

~

Less than ten minutes later, Delman, Dexter, Dr. Matsumoto, and Marlow were all sitting on one side of a table facing off against two government agents from a security department whose three-letter acronym was apparently a state secret. They wore jet black suits, which seemed to absorb all light—just like their expressions. Several more agents had fanned out across the various departments within the organization, asking questions and poking their noses into every nook and cranny. Delman was glad he had retrieved and reset his AI glasses as he would need all the help he could get in reading between the lines of this conversation.

"So you're saying this woman can talk to machines?" said Agent Hegarty, the presumptive leader of this cadre of spooks.

"Not talk, not verbally. She does so by thought alone. And not any machine, it has to have an intelligence component, some level of AI," replied Delman.

"Wow. Did you hear that, Agent Wiseman?" He directed this at his colleague.

"I sure did," he replied.

"She can talk to machines," Hegarty repeated. "What do you think of that?"

"Weird, is what I think."

Agent Hegarty fixed his gaze back on Delman. "So you're saying, that you just let this... machine whisperer walk out of here, without so much as an, 'excuse me miss, but where do you think you're going?'"

"There was a riot going on, the HQ building had been infiltrated, we had to invoke our evacuation protocol," Marlow explained.

"Did you hear that Agent Wiseman? They have protocols."

"Everyone should have a protocol. That's what I always say."

Delman's head was spinning again, but not from alcohol, it was from listening to this ludicrous clown act. He couldn't make sense of it, nor was his personal AI any help. It was just as confused as he was. "So are you going to try and find her?" he said, more out of desperation than anything else.

"Well gee, there's an idea," said Agent Hegarty.

"Genius. I see why they pay you the big bucks," added Agent Wiseman.

"Do you guys take anything seriously?" Delman exploded, clearly sick of this carry-on. "Maybe you two would be better off doing stand-up."

The mood in the room took a noticeable downturn, like a sudden decompression. There was a pause as the two agents took a moment to consider this insult.

"We'll keep that in mind." Agent Hegarty finally said. "If this national security thing of protecting our great country from the nefarious activities of our enemies, and the juvenile incompetence of our own industrialists doesn't work out... I'll make sure to remember your advice."

"Absolutely," said Agent Wiseman. "Everyone needs a plan B. That's what I always say."

After a tense moment, Hegarty continued his questioning. "Anything else she can do that we should know about?"

Delman hesitated, not sure how much he should tell these goons. But the reality was, they were now the only viable chance they had of finding Dawn Harrison. And, like it or not, he needed them. The last thing Delman wanted now was to give the national security vultures another excuse to take over their research. Best to do as Dexter had directed, play ball, don't try and hide anything.

"Eh... she may also have augmented cognition."

"I assume by that, you mean she's smarter than the average bear," said Hegarty.

"Eh... that's not necessarily the case," Dr. Matsumoto interrupted.

"Well which is it—smart or stupid?" Hegarty asked.

"She has an AI implanted in her brain, but it has been dialed down due to, eh... an adverse reaction. However, it may activate under certain circumstances."

"Aren't you guys just full of surprises," said Hegarty. "So when does this bag of tricks explode in her head?"

"Had she still been under our supervision," Dr. Matsumoto began, casting a cold glance at Delman, "then we would have nurtured her abilities to 'talk to machines', as you so eloquently put it, Agent Hegarty. Once she reached a certain proficiency and comfort with the neural interaction, then the internal AI would come on-stream and she would potentially have vastly increased cognitive abilities, superior to any human alive."

"I see," said Hegarty scratching his chin and seeming genuinely amazed by this revelation. "That's quite a thing to give to someone who—if my understanding is correct—is an ex-alcoholic. Quite a thing, don't you think, Agent Wiseman?"

"Quite a thing, Agent Hegarty."

"A side effect of the procedure is curing addictions," Dr. Matsumoto explained. "It's the reason why she was legally allowed to participate. She was also clean for over twenty-four months beforehand. Notwithstanding the fact that she is very fit and healthy, and went into this with her eyes open."

"Except, I hear she's lost her memory in the process," said Hegarty.

"A temporary condition, I assure you," said Dr. Matsumoto.

Delman raised a hand. "Look, what we do here is... well sensitive, as you are no doubt fully aware of. Our concern is her safe return, always has been."

Agent Hegarty gave a long sigh followed by a quick nod, as if he had come to some major conclusion in his head. "Very well," he said finally. Then, he pulled a phone out of his pocket and started flicking at the screen. "Do you recognize this guy?" He passed the phone to Delman.

"That's... Prince Waleed bin Saeed's bodyguard."

"It is. And a former Tiger Squad hitman. A nasty piece of work, but very capable."

"You're not suggesting... the Saudis are involved." Delman could feel his grip on the Neuromorph slipping away.

"Clearly your data security has been compromised, probably during the riot," said Hegarty.

"We did a very thorough sweep of the building after. I assure you we found everything there was to find," said Marlow, clearly taking umbrage at the suggestion he and his team were less than professional.

"This building, but what about the bio-chip facility?" Hegarty jerked his head in the general direction.

All eyes turned to Jeb Marlow. "Eh, that wasn't affected by the rioters."

Agent Hegarty sat forward. "I think it's time we took a closer look at your Saudi friends. We may find that they have been up to more than simply investing."

# CHAPTER 20
# FISHERMAN'S WHARF

D awn Harrison abducted, Tyler and Ethan dead. Marlow couldn't believe the absolute shitstorm that was now going down. The entire Neuromorph campus was swarming with National Security Agency people, looking into every electron that moved in the corporation's network. His own security sweep after the riot now looked pathetically incompetent in comparison to the deep forensic analysis that was currently underway. He wondered if he still had a job. What use was he now?

He thought of Harrison, the woman from the gym, the one he wanted to ask on a date, and wondered what she must be going through. He thought of Tyler and Ethan, both lying on a cold slab in the city morgue. He felt angry, he felt frustrated, but most of all he felt responsible. It was he who persuaded the two security contractors to take the job, and now they were dead and Harrison was nowhere to be found. He needed to do something, anything, to find out who did the hit and make them pay. He reached into his pocket to get his phone only to remember that the NSA agents had taken it for forensic examination. He lifted the receiver on the old handset on his desk and called the San Francisco Police Department. After a few moments of being shunted around and listening to elevator music, he finally got connected to Bill Flaherty, his old boss.

"I shouldn't be talking to you, Jeb," Flaherty said as soon as he answered.

"Tyler and Ethan, what can you tell me?" Jeb asked.

There was a pause, followed by a long intake of breath, followed by the sound of a door closing. "Can't talk here. Meet me down by the Pier, the usual spot."

"Okay, on my way."

～

An hour later, Marlow spotted Flaherty leaning against the wooden railing, looking out to sea, and smoking a cigarette. He came up beside him. Flaherty didn't look at him, but simply pointed out to sea over at a couple of pontoons that had been taken over by a colony of sea lions.

"They don't know how lucky they are, lying around in the sun all day long. Not a worry in the world."

Marlow nodded. "Yeah." Then turned to look at his old boss. "So what can you tell me about Tyler and Ethan? How's the investigation going?"

"Can't tell you nothing, 'cause it's out of our hands, Jeb," Flaherty said. "Someone with some serious clout has shut down the investigation." He flicked the cigarette butt into the sea. "I assume it's the same guys that are now crawling all over your new employer."

"Listen, they were doing a job for me, Tyler and Ethan," Marlow said. "It was me who put them in harm's way. So I'd like to find the bastard who did this. You must have found out something before they shut it down?"

"We'd all like to find whoever did it, they were ex-cops after all," Flaherty lit another cigarette. "But I don't know what you guys have gotten yourselves into over there, but it ain't something that the Department is allowed to touch. Nothing I can do. Sorry, Jeb."

Marlow gave a long sigh. "Okay, I get it. It was a long shot anyway."

"It's not like the old days, Jeb, back when you were there. Now we can't do nothing without the AI giving us the go-ahead. A case comes in and before anyone does a damn thing it's run through the algorithms. Then whatever it spits out, that's what we do. No real investigators anymore, Jeb," he shook his head. "The damn thing knows what you're doing, what you're thinking. Heck, it even knows what you're going to do before you know it yourself."

"Yeah, it can seem that way," Marlow agreed. "But I think you can never really know a person until you tie them to a chair and punch them in the face a few times."

Flaherty threw his head back and laughed. "Ha, can't see the AI ever doing that."

"Not yet anyway," said Marlow.

"Seems to me, Jeb, we're all just becoming slaves to the AI. Nothing more than the fleshy hand of the machine."

"That's a good one, Bill. I must remember that."

"I'm sure you already know where all this AI business is taking us, what with you working for the Neuromorph Corporation."

"Yeah, you would think so," Marlow said. "But ironically, all I am is a glorified HR manager, Bill. I spend most of my time working out staff schedules; who's out sick, who wants time off for a wedding, who's on the lam."

"Still, I bet the money's good?"

Marlow grinned, "Sure, but it would wanna be, having to put up with a bunch of paranoid tech bros all day long."

They were silent for a moment as they watched the sea lions loll about on the pontoons.

"I heard the boys are heading to O'Malley's this evening, having a drink for Tyler and Ethan," Marlow said.

"Yeah, but if you're thinking of going then don't be surprised if you get a cold reception," Flaherty cautioned.

Marlow looked over at his old boss. "Why, because they were on a job for me?"

"No, not that. It's because you work for the enemy. The AI that's taken over the department belongs to the Neuromorph Corporation. Some of the boys are having a hard time adjusting. I can tell you there was a lot of cheering when that riot broke out. A few of them would secretly like to see the whole place burned to the ground."

"I can't say I blame them. Soon we'll all be out of a job," Marlow sighed.

"There's one thing I can tell you, Jeb." Flaherty's tone became serious. "It's a word of warning. These people that killed Tyler and Ethan are dangerous, very dangerous, not like the usual scumbags that we deal with. So you be careful about getting involved." He took a deep breath, "Anyway, it was good to catch up. I best get back or the AI will dock my pay for slacking off," he grinned, then walked away.

Marlow stood there for a while just watching the sea lions and the tourists. Then his phone rang. He fished it out of his pocket and stared at the screen wondering who the heck could be calling him since he had only just bought it a half hour ago, no one knew the number, and he hadn't even used it yet. *Spam call,* he thought. Yet, out of curiosity, he hit accept and put it up to his ear. "Yeah?"

"Marlow, this is Agent Hegarty. I think it's time you and I had a little talk. If you're finished chatting with your old Department boss, then meet me back in the Operations Center in Neuromorph."

# CHAPTER 21
# PARANOIA

M arlow stood for a moment and surveyed the complete takeover of his former Security Operations Room at Neuromorph by Agent Hegarty and his team of NSA operatives. They had piled into the campus, sweeping through every sector and department, forensically investigating every bit and byte in the entire facility. The room was now populated by a raft of hastily assembled workstations, wall monitors, satellite feeds, server racks, and God knows what else. Each under the watchful eye of an army of black-suited clones: dull, expressionless, and completely devoid of personality. Marlow suspected they must have a secret lab somewhere, where they were manufactured.

Hegarty spotted him entering and called him over to a workstation.

"Jeb Marlow," he said by way of a greeting. "I want you to have a listen to this." He nodded to a tech who tapped a few keys on a keyboard and a voice recording began. It was Marlow's voice—directing the two security contractors to the parking garage where they met their untimely death.

"That's... that's not me. I never said that," Marlow looked over at the agent in horror.

Hegarty raised a hand. "Relax, we know it wasn't you." He picked up Marlow's old cellphone, the one confiscated for analysis by his team of minions.

"Your phone was compromised." He waved it in the air. "As were most of the devices of those attending the Saudi investment tour of the bio-server building."

Marlow's mouth dropped open. "H... How?" he stammered.

"A very sophisticated, near-field communications hack. It had been considered theoretically possible but we've never seen it out in the wild before. They even compromised Harry Delman's AI." He reached down and picked up the CEO's AI glasses from the workbench, turning them this way and that in his hand.

"How did you manage to pry those away from him?" Marlow asked, surprised. "I don't know how many times I've tried to do a security scan, but he refuses. Last time I tried, he threatened to fire me."

"We have our ways," Hegarty grinned. "But he's not taking it very well. Rumor has it that he's locked himself away on his yacht, suffering from reality overload syndrome."

"Yeah, that sounds about right." Marlow nodded.

Hegarty turned to the tech again. "Show the brother's house."

A photograph blossomed onto the monitor showing a well-to-do street. It looked to have been taken by a fisheye lens, possibly from a domestic security system.

"This is from a camera at the subject's brother's house, the morning she was picked up."

"She does have a name, you know." Marlow gave an exasperated sigh.

"You knew her, didn't you?" Hegarty sounded like a judge seeking clarity.

"Well, yes, eh... sort of. I'd seen her a few times at the gym, training people. This was a few months back. But I assume you know all that."

Hegarty was silent for a beat, then turned back to the image on screen. "You see that?" he pointed at a black van partially hidden by a blur of foliage. "That's our man."

Marlow leaned in, but there was not much detail in the image.

"Malik Al-Sayf, the prince's bodyguard, ex-Tiger Squad. He knew where and when to find the subject. Then used an AI to clone your voice and redirect the security contractors to the kill zone."

"What's Tiger Squad?" Marlow had heard Hegarty mention this at the initial meeting but had no idea what it was.

"The Saudi version of Mossad. Very capable, very deadly. Rumored to be behind the assassination of several people deemed problematic for the state's rulers," Hegarty explained.

"You're saying the Saudis are behind this?"

"No. I'm not saying that. What I am saying is that your old boss, Flaherty, is right. These are very dangerous people. Not something you want to get yourself mixed up in."

"Well, I already am mixed up in it." Marlow stiffened his stance. "Those were my guys. I got them into it, persuaded them to take on the job."

"I get it. You were all buddies in the Department back in the day and it's in your blood to go do something about their murder. But this is not about them." He fixed Marlow with a cold stare. "It's not even about the woman, Harrison. It's about an extremely valuable item of technology that absolutely cannot fall into the wrong hands. This is about the security of this country and I do not need a lone wolf trying to be a hero. Because you *will* get yourself killed."

Marlow opened his hands in a gesture of appeal. "So the people don't matter?"

"You're not seeing the big picture here." Hegarty now sounded like an avuncular headmaster, admonishing an errant teacher. "This is a war. One that's waged on the AI level. Whoever has the best tech, wins. At the moment, that's us and we need to protect that advantage, at all costs."

Marlow looked around at all the NSA techs that populated the operations room, and he could feel some of the fight drain away from him. Hegarty was right, of course. This was a high-tech battle fought on a level far beyond human intelligence. What hope did he have in contributing anything that would help nail this Malik guy, never mind getting Dawn Harrison back in one piece.

"You need to accept that you're in over your head." Hegarty continued. "There have been many security failures here, Jeb. But, there's a big difference between being incompetent and being outclassed. Your failure, if you want to call it that, is insufficient paranoia."

"Paranoia?" Marlow raised his eyebrows.

"You couldn't conceive of the protest turning into a riot as it had never happened before. You couldn't conceive of comms devices being hacked, since they were all locked away safely in a Faraday cage. Yet, both these things happened and both are connected. Our good luck in all of this, if you want to call it that, was that the subject decided to do a runner. Only for that, the hack might never have been exposed in time."

Marlow sighed. "So what now?"

"Paranoia," Hegarty continued, ignoring Marlow's question, "is what AI is very good at. Like a grandmaster, it sees all the moves, not just the obvious ones, but all those moves that we can't even conceive of. That's why we leave the thinking to the AI. Because that's what the other side is doing to us."

"That all sounds wonderful," said Marlow, his tone cynical, "but have you dug up any leads on her current whereabouts?"

Hegarty laughed. "Ha, always the investigator. You are wasted in this job... as a glorified HR manager." He fixed him with a knowing look.

Marlow realized that the agent had heard every last word of the conversation with Bill Flaherty at the wharf, a place that he thought was safe from eavesdropping. Hegarty was right, of course. He really wasn't paranoid enough.

"To answer your question, yes we have... leads. And the AI is running the numbers on where she's probably going to pop up next. So don't you worry, we'll find her."

"Well then, thanks for the update. Let's do it again sometime." Marlow turned to go.

"Before you go. I have something for you."

Marlow turned back and sighed. "Okay, shoot."

Hegarty cast his gaze across the busy operations center. "If we are to stay one step ahead in this war then we need more than just paranoia. There are also times when we need to tie someone to a chair and punch them in the face." He looked back at Marlow.

Marlow wasn't sure what the agent was getting at. He swept a hand around at the NSA techs. "Well, I don't see any of these guys doing that."

"Ha, you're absolutely right. These people have not been engineered for social interaction."

"No kidding!" Marlow wondered if Hegarty was actually being serious or not. "So what are you saying to me?"

"I had a look into your background in the Department. Very impressive."

"And very badly paid," Marlow added.

Hegarty gave him a considered look. "If, during the course of our work in protecting this great country of ours, we come across a particular individual, in a particular circumstance, with a particular skill set, we make an approach."

"So... you're offering me a job?" Marlow couldn't believe what he was hearing after all the admonishment over his failures.

"What we are offering you is an opportunity, Jeb. An opportunity that better utilizes your skills as a field operative.

'The fleshy hand of the machine,' I think was how your boss put it?"

Marlow's brain couldn't process this, not now, it was too absurd. "I already have a job. Head of Security at Neuromorph."

"Yes, well you'll find that's my job now," Hegarty smiled.

Marlow felt he was being pushed into a corner, being checkmated, outsmarted, yet again. "I'll... need to think about it."

"No problem. Just don't take too long."

He turned to go.

"And remember. Paranoia is your friend," Hegarty called out to him as he left.

Marlow nodded. "Paranoia. Got it."

# CHAPTER 22
# CONTINGENCY

alik withdrew the card from the pump—it was a burner, untraceable. Already a few people had come over to see what was going on. He moved back toward the van door but kept his cool and tried to make it sound like the drone had just randomly crashed. Just some idiot who had lost control of his toy.

Someone toed the broken machine where it lay on the ground. "Some of these kids just don't know how dangerous these things can be." He shook his head and then looked around as if trying to find the errant operator.

"Yeah, I heard some of these morons were buzzing flights taking off at the airport over in Oakland. Crazy stuff," said another.

"I heard they brought in a couple of falconers. They're using eagles to take them down."

GERALD M. KILBY

"No way?"

"You okay, mister?"

Malik nodded. "All good. Thanks. Anyway, I best get back to work. I suppose I should gather this up and bring it over to the station."

"Yeah, like they're going to do anything."

"Still, probably best I report it."

He gathered up the remains of the drone and clambered into the driver's seat of the van, dumping the dead drone in the passenger seat footwell. He started the engine and waved to his new friends as he moved out of the gas station and back onto the main road. He kept his speed below the limit—no need to draw any more attention than was necessary. After a minute or so, he settled down and thought about what had just happened.

Malik flicked a glance at the shattered drone; it didn't look anything special, not military, not special forces, just a pretty standard domestic drone with a few modifications, mainly the puny taser. Yet, it didn't look homemade. Perhaps it was a prototype, something experimental. But the more important question in Malik's mind was, who was controlling it?

He turned around and took a look at the woman in the back. She was still lying face down on the floor. Visions of the TikTok video, with her controlling a drone, came into his mind. *No,* he thought. *It's not possible, is it?*

Then again, maybe he had simply been rumbled for doing the hit on the two Neuromorph contractors. Did someone witness it? But if that were the case, then there would be a trail of cop cars after him, all squawking and flashing lights, and a chopper in the air with a sniper ready to take the shot. On the other hand, maybe it was just some weird random thing. Some drone that lost its control signal and went berserk. Yet, the more he thought about it, the less sense it made and the more unsettled he became.

He stopped for a moment at a traffic junction and looked back at his captive again. She was now lying on her side, still and quiet. *Was she controlling that drone with her mind?* he wondered. He couldn't bring himself to believe it. It was not possible; he was pretty sure that TikTok video was a fake. So what, if his handlers were dumb enough to believe it? Anyway, it didn't matter in the end—it had failed. He glanced down at the remains of the little drone.

Nevertheless, he couldn't just ignore it; he needed a contingency. At a minimum, he needed to switch vehicles as soon as possible. Malik fished his cellphone out of his pocket and sent a message to his handler. Ideally, he would have preferred to go directly to the handover location, but the bizarre nature of the drone attack convinced him that he had to change his plan. He spoke in Arabic, assuming that his captive wouldn't understand. It would, of course, be translated in real-time into Mandarin. He quickly outlined the bizarre attack by the taser drone at the gas station and requested an immediate vehicle switch.

A moment later, he got a pin with a set of coordinates along with a request to head to that location, lie low, and await further instructions. Malik pulled up to the side of the road, booted up his laptop, and opened a highly secure GPS navigation app on the laptop screen. The pin he had been sent redirected him to an old abandoned airfield, around an hour and a half drive away.

From the rear of the van, he could hear his captive moan a few times. He glanced back at her, slightly concerned. She seemed to bury her head into her chest, rocking it back and forth... weird. He hoped she wasn't going to be sick, because with her mouth taped up, there was a high chance she could choke. But she seemed to settle down, and since time was critical, he decided he would risk leaving it on. The last thing he needed now was for her to start screaming and shouting as soon as he ripped off the duct tape. He had learned that lesson the hard way a few times before. People who were as quiet as the night until you took the gag off. Then they suddenly found their lungs—until he put a bullet through their brain. But he had to deliver this package clean and whole... mostly. So best leave the gag on for now. He put the van into drive and got back on the road.

The navigation app on the laptop charted his route in a constantly adjusting blue line. But he didn't really need it as he knew exactly where they were taking him. He had been to this old airfield before. It wasn't completely abandoned; there were still a few old geezers that ran small, part-time workshops there. One of whom Malik had reason to use in the past. For a price, he could make a vehicle disappear, no questions asked. Perhaps his Chinese friends were using the same guy, although maybe not, as the location they gave him was an old abandoned hangar quite a distance away from any activity.

He glanced down a few times at the laptop screen, not to check his route but because it seemed to be glitching. The screen would flicker and dim, then settle down again. He hoped the computer was not on the blink because it was a vital link for his handlers. He reached over and shut it down just in case it was overheating or something. He'd check it again later.

A few moments after that, he noticed his captive had also settled down, no more moaning and groaning.

# CHAPTER 23
# DAVINCI BRIDGE

D awn's muscles ached, her shoulders, arms, back—in fact, her entire body was feeling the strain from the constricted position she had been lying in this whole time. She tried several exercises, moving her arms and body as much as she could to keep the blood flowing. It was difficult and at times painful. Nevertheless, she tried to stay calm, keep her breathing steady, and focus on relaxing.

Then her brain started that weird tingling again. But this time she took it as a potential opportunity; some device had just activated and she was determined to try and figure it out. She forgot about her aching muscles and concentrated her mind on the signal.

At times, she could visualize a computer screen, even decipher an image of a map of some kind. Yet she couldn't quite discern the fine detail, nor could she affect any meaningful interaction with the system no matter how much she tried. In the end, the tingling stopped just as quickly as it had started. She assumed that her abductor had switched off his laptop. Dawn was frustrated but clung to the hope that she might get another chance to get a message out.

For the next half hour or so, she wondered if what they had put in her head was even designed for interfacing with such devices. What she had experienced so far, from the very first moment she woke up in the hospital bed, was clearly two-way communication with an AI. Maybe she was pushing the boundaries of what was possible with this new, weird superpower she seemed to possess.

Dawn was just about reaching the limits of her physical endurance when the van turned off the main road, bumped along an old worn track for a short distance, and rolled to a stop. She heard the guy getting out and the sound of large metal garage doors being opened. He got back in and drove the vehicle into a huge workshop building of some sort. After the van had parked, he got out, opened the back of the van, and dragged Dawn out.

As she looked around, she could see that she was in an old airplane hangar. There were two huge sliding doors, along with a dilapidated workshop area and the clutter of old light aircraft parts. He pulled out an intimidating-looking hunting knife and cut the zip ties that bound her ankles together. She tried to take a moment to stretch her legs, but already he was leading her across to the other side of the hangar where there was a row of small offices. He pushed her through the door of one of the offices—a bare, empty space. He sat her down on an upturned wooden crate and ripped the duct tape from her mouth, then cut the zip ties on her wrists.

He stood over her holding the knife close to her face. "I would prefer if you stayed quiet," he said very slowly and deliberately. "You can scream and shout as much as you like, but there isn't anyone around here to hear you, so please don't waste your time. We'll be here for a while, so you'd better get comfortable."

From a bag, he pulled out a bottle of water and a store-bought sandwich and threw them in her lap. "Here," he said with a grunt. "And don't say I never gave you anything." He grinned and walked out. Dawn could hear a bolt being thrown on the far side of the door.

She stood up and stretched her back and shoulders, and began pacing around the room swinging her arms trying to get some feeling back into them. The room was about the size of a school classroom. Old, with wood paneling along the sides, much of which had fallen off and lay in heaps here and there. Apart from that, the only other things in the room were an old wooden crate, a few scraps of cardboard, several fallen ceiling tiles, and a huge quantity of dust and cobwebs. Along one wall was a row of cracked and broken windows looking out across a desolate airfield. Evening was coming and the sky was growing darker. She peered out and thought she saw some lights off in the distance on the far end of the landing strip. But even with the glass broken, there was no getting through the heavy security grill embedded into the concrete on the outside. Another row of windows ran along the opposite side of the room. These were mostly intact and looked out into the hangar area. She could see her abductor busying himself taking some stuff out of the van and dropping it on a workbench. There was no getting out of here that she could see.

Eventually, Dawn began to eat her simple meal and wondered what the heck she was going to do now. She had been reckless with the little drone, expected too much from it, even after it had advised her on the best course of action. Now it was dead, a part of her felt a little guilty for having killed it. Sure, it was only a machine, but she had begun to have some affinity for the quirky little thing, and now... well, it was no more.

Her head began to tingle again and she reckoned her abductor must have booted up his laptop. She peered through the grimy window and could see him sitting with his back to her, laptop open. She concentrated. Maybe if she could figure this out, she might be able to use it to send a message. It was a heck of a long shot, yet there was nothing else she could do. She had to try.

It was the same as when she had attempted this back in the van—a vague visual image in her mind of a computer screen which would fade in and out of clarity depending on her focus. She dug deep, zoning in on the source, and began to gain clarity. It was a video call, from someone called Mandy Max. *Weird*, she thought, *he's not on some porn chat, is he? Maybe she had gotten him all hot and bothered, being tied up and bound in the back of the van?*

Suddenly a voice resonated in her head, loud and clear.

*'Hello, it's Morph here, your personal AI assistant. How can I help today?'*

Dawn almost stumbled. She had to put a hand out and grab the wall to steady herself. For a moment she thought it might be coming from the video call on the laptop. But this was crystal clear, hi-fidelity—coming from right inside her head.

*'Eh... Morph?'* she answered.

*'Yes, Morph, your personal AI assistant. Sorry I could not talk to you since our first interaction, but you had not yet reached the required competence with the cranial implant for my services to be activated before now.'*

*'What? From the lab?'* Dawn was confused. Was this the same thing that had talked to her back when she first woke up in Neuromorph?

*'Kind of,'* it replied. *'I'm a subset of the general purpose Neuromorph AI model, which has been integrated into your implant to enable cognitive augmentation.'*

*'I have an AI in my head?'*

*'In a word, yes.'*

Dawn began to feel slightly queasy, maybe it was the sandwich—she never checked the date—or maybe the entire ordeal was just catching up with her. Either way, she stumbled back to the wooden crate and sat down.

*'Can you send a message? Can you call the cops?'* Having a personal AI buried in her skull was all well and good, but only if it was useful for more than just telling her the height of the Empire State Building or the distance from San Francisco to Tokyo.

*'Sorry, there is no accessible Wi-Fi in range.'*

*'Well, a fat lot of good you are to me now. And why didn't you show up before, when I could have used the help?'*

'I'm very sorry, but you first needed to display a certain level of competency with the interface implant.'

Dawn was silent for a moment as she took another swig of water from the bottle. What Morph was saying to her kinda made sense, in a way. She was not freaking out, not like the first time. Having an AI in her head seemed... well, okay. Weird, but okay. Had this thing started talking to her from day one, then maybe she would have gone completely mad. But now, it seemed like a natural progression—if you consider having a mind–machine interface drilled into your skull natural.

'What about that guy out there, on the porn chat. He must have a connection?' Dawn suggested.

'He does, but I can't access it. The encryption is too strong. Oh, and by the way, just so you know, he's not on a porn chat. He's discussing the estimated arrival time of his replacement van.'

Dawn sat up. 'You can read that?'

'I'm simply interpreting the information you were able to decipher via your implant interface.'

'I see,' she mused, even though she really didn't. 'How long will it be, this new van?'

'They estimate four hours.'

Dawn relaxed a little, she had some time before the next phase of her ordeal would begin. 'There has to be a way out of here?'

'I'd be happy to help with that,' Morph replied, as if it were helping with washing up. 'Please look around the room so that I can analyze the visual data. I'm sure I can make some recommendations.'

Dawn shifted her focus to various parts of the room; the

barred windows, the piles of rotten wood paneling, the door. As she did, Morph rattled off a ream of useless data; air volume, ambient temperature, wood species, weight of materials... all completely useless to her. That is, until she looked above her.

There was an old-fashioned false ceiling constructed with square tiles, many of which had fallen down and lay scattered on the floor. Above this, through the many gaping holes, she could see a confusion of ducts, pipes, and electrical conduit.

*'Industrial air ventilation ducting, galvanized steel, most likely running throughout the building. The square area of the opening should be sufficient to accommodate your physical frame. I conclude that your best option for escape is to remove the vent cover on that ducting above the doorway, climb in, and crawl to another area within the building that enables you to exit without being seen.'*

Dawn studied the ducting with renewed interest. It didn't look inviting, it was dark and dingy. But it was a potential way out. *'Hmm... that might actually work, Morph.'*

*'No problem, my pleasure, I'm here to assist.'*

Dawn took a moment to consider just what was going on here. She was talking to an AI embedded in her brain, or so she believed. Yet, how would she know if she was not simply going mad, and making up an imaginary friend to help her in a highly stressful situation? *Does it matter,* she wondered. *If it helps me get out of here, then so what. I can just get some counseling on the other side.*

*'Slight problem, Morph,'* she said. *'I can't reach it. Not even standing on that crate.'*

*'You could use some of those lengths of wood paneling that have fallen off the walls,'* Morph suggested.

Dawn looked at this pathetic pile of wood—strips around four feet long, not very thick, and some were even rotten in places. She could not figure out how even stacking them all together, one on top of the other, would give her enough height to reach the vent. *'I can't see how any of these are going to help,'* she replied.

*'You can construct a da Vinci bridge,'* Morph answered in a tone that implied this should be obvious to anyone, even without an AI implanted in their brain.

*'Uh... what's that?'* Dawn had no idea.

*'No problem, I'll show you. Just follow my instructions.'*

Over the next few minutes, the AI directed Dawn in the construction of a da Vinci bridge. It consisted of an intersecting, intricate lattice work that, when finished, gave her a three-foot platform on which to place the crate. She stood back to admire her work, although it looked pretty flimsy to her eye. The AI informed her that the type of wood was elm, common in these parts, and used for construction during the period in which this aircraft hangar would have been built. And that its strength would be more than adequate to support her. It was at this point that Dawn finally realized she was not going crazy, because there was absolutely no way on earth she could have come up with this solution on her own. She really did have an AI friend rattling around in her head.

Dawn pulled off the vent cover, dropping it down onto a pile of old cardboard to muffle the sound. She peered into the gaping maw of the ducting. It was just as she expected: dark and dingy, with an oversupply of dead rats. She climbed in and was instantly assailed by a stench and a cloud of dust that rose up and enveloped her. She started to gag and cough as she shuffled her way forward.

*'I can't see a damn thing,'* said Dawn after she had gone only a few feet, still unsure if the old ventilation system would hold her weight.

*'If my analysis is correct, and it always is, then taking a direct path forward should bring you to what was originally the reception area for the aircraft hangar. There should be another vent there where you can drop down, and then try to access the front door.'*

Dawn inched forward, hoping that the AI wasn't simply guessing. The duct creaked and buckled as she moved. She took it slow, trying to minimize noise. After what seemed like an eternity for her, she found the next vent cover, quietly removed it and dropped down into a cluttered room that had been a reception area at some point in its history. She moved quietly across to the front door, hoping that it wouldn't be padlocked on the outside. Fortunately, it had been bolted from the inside, so with a little effort and a fair amount of muffled grunting, she freed the rusty bolt. Then she pulled hard on the door to crack it open. Eventually, she had a gap just wide enough for her to squeeze through and out into the cool of the night. She took a moment to take a few breaths, clear the dust from her lungs, and get her bearings.

Across the dark expanse of the abandoned airfield, a glimmer of light emanated from a far-off building. It gave her hope. She would head toward it, and maybe find a phone where she could call the cops. She pulled the hood up around her shaved head, which was feeling the early night's chill, and started walking.

# CHAPTER 24
# DYING TO MEET

The evening temperature was dropping, currently hovering around fifty-three degrees, and the time was exactly 8:17 PM, or so Morph, her new AI friend, informed her. Under any other circumstances, Dawn would have been nothing short of petrified at the sudden manifestation of this artificial intelligence inside her head. Yet, as she made her way across the abandoned airfield, she imagined herself at some elegant dinner party where she could not only amaze the other guests with her encyclopedic knowledge but, better still, take on those pompous assholes who always populate these gatherings, chopping them down to size with a blizzard of facts and carefully considered analysis. This fantasy, this daydream she was having, seemed to suddenly unlock a torrent of past memories. Flashes of party nights in expensive places with expensive people exploded in her mind. It was enough to stop her dead in her tracks.

She had been focused on making her way as fast as possible toward the glow of lights coming from the building on the far side of the airfield. This meant directly crossing the old runway with no cover and being completely exposed. Stopping here, right out in the open, was not a wise move. But the flood of memories had her physically frozen on the spot. The scenes were filled with laughing, joyous people, dancing, swimming, drinking... there was a lot of drinking... and as she sifted through each memory, new connections were being made, faces she thought she recognized, but yet couldn't put names to.

'My apologies for interrupting your private thoughts,' Morph's voice cut through in her mind, 'but this is not the best location to reminisce about your past life, considering the lengths you have gone to, to extract yourself from the hangar building.'

So deep were her thoughts that she had almost forgotten about the AI.

'Eh, yes... better keep going.'

She focused her attention back toward the lights, this time with renewed hope. It seemed there was a possibility that she could regain the memory of who she had been. All she needed to do was to get out of this situation and back to safety. The glow from the workshop pulled her forward. As she got closer, she could see it was a mechanic's workshop; the big roller shutter doors on the front were retracted all the way up and she could see a number of vehicles in various states of disassembly. Leaning over the hood of one of these was an old guy in a pair of ratty overalls.

Dawn cautiously approached, stopping outside the wide,

open door of the workshop, and called in to the mechanic, "Hello?"

For a moment, it seemed as if he hadn't heard her. Then all of a sudden, he stood upright and flipped around to look at her. He was pointing a handgun at her. "Who the hell are you?"

"Woah, easy there." Dawn raised her hands in the air. "I just need to use your phone. I need to call the cops."

"The cops, eh? Can't say I'd be happy with a bunch of those guys nosing around here." He kept the gun pointed at her.

"Please, I've been abducted... tied up over at that old aircraft hangar." She pointed back over the far side of the airfield. "I managed to escape, now I really need to call the authorities."

The old guy moved forward, still keeping his weapon on her, and looked across at the dull outline of the hangar in the distance. "The old Knox hangar, you say?"

"Yeah. Look, I just need to get the hell out of here."

"So how many are over there?" he asked.

"Just one. A man, Arab, I think."

The old guy seemed to think for a moment. "Arab, you say?"

"Yeah, I think he spoke Arabic. He's definitely Middle Eastern."

The old guy pursed his lips and lowered the weapon. "I got an old landline in the office over there. You can go call from that." He gestured over at a small enclosed room at the back of the workshop.

Dawn slowly lowered her hands and began moving toward it. "Thanks. I really appreciate this."

"Yeah, sure," he grunted in reply, still keeping his gaze on the hangar at the far edge of the airfield.

Inside the office was a mess of old papers, manuals, car parts, empty food cartons, dead bugs, cigarette butts, and beer cans, all covered in a layer of dust and oil. Dawn swept her gaze around this mess searching for an old phone. She couldn't find any. *'Where the heck is it?'* she asked in her mind.

*'I too have failed to identify a fixed-line telecommunication receiver anywhere within all this mess,'* answered Morph.

Dawn turned around to go back out and ask him where it was hidden, but to her surprise she found the old guy shutting the office door and locking her in. She rushed over in panic, only to find it firmly bolted. She looked out the side window into the workshop area. The old guy was talking into a cellphone.

He looked over at her. "Sorry, ma'am," he shouted. "But like I said, don't want no cops snooping around here causing a fuss."

"You bastard, let me out." Dawn rattled the door handle. But it didn't budge.

*'Help me, Morph. What do I do?'*

*'Throw the office chair through the window, then use that crowbar lying on the bench to clear the broken glass from the edges so you don't cut yourself climbing through it. The explosive impact of the chair going through the window will stun the old mechanic for a second, and the crowbar will make for an intimidating bludgeoning implement.'*

Dawn didn't think twice about this course of action. Her blood was up, she was sick and tired of being harassed. She was raging inside... borderline berserk.

The heavy office chair arced through the air, smashed through the window in an explosion of shattering glass, and continued on into the workshop, trailing a tangle of window blinds and flashing shards. Before it even hit the floor, Dawn was already through, crowbar in hand.

Morph was half-right, the old guy was caught off guard, but he still had the wits to pull the handgun out and fire off a shot that hit the floor in front of her.

"Don't fucking move, or I'll put one through your pretty little head."

Dawn froze. *'Crap, what now?'*

*'You could run, but he will try to shoot you, and he may get lucky. Best course of action is to de-escalate and wait for an opportunity to overpower him.'*

Dawn shook her head and sighed. She turned back around to face the old guy, slowly raising her hands. She could see that he was still rattled, and there was a shake in his gun hand.

*'Feign surrender, put down the crowbar, and get in close to him. He can't move back as he is right up against that stack of pallets. Your reaction time is considerably faster than his, and there is a considerable quantity of adrenaline coursing through your bloodstream that will compound your strength.'*

She looked directly at the old guy. "Okay, let's just take a breath here, no one needs to get hurt." She moved in closer. "I'm putting down the crowbar." She placed it on the roof of the car he had been working on, moving closer still. "Maybe there's a way we can work things out."

*'Another pace forward then grab his right gun wrist with your right hand, tight, push the gun away and swing inside with your back to him, pin him against the pallets, and slam your left elbow up under his jaw.'*

Dawn kept her hands palms out in a gesture of appeasement and took another step closer. She could see his weapon dropping a little. Then she struck, exactly as Morph had outlined. She grabbed his wrist and twisted her body. A shot discharged, burying itself harmlessly in the workshop floor. She pinned him back and slammed her elbow into his jaw as hard as she could. He crumpled on the floor like a rag doll. The handgun fell out of his hand and blood oozed from his mouth where he must have bitten his lip.

'Oh no. Did I just kill him?'

'No, he's unconscious,' Morph assured her.

Dawn was relieved. Much as she detested this old bastard, she didn't want to kill anyone. She picked up the gun and dropped it into an open barrel of used engine oil—just in case he came to before she managed to get out of here.

"Don't move a muscle," a familiar, heavily accented voice called out from the doorway. Dawn slowly tilted her head to see her abductor aiming a silenced pistol at her, gripped with both hands, a demonic look of intent in his eyes.

'Damnit, what do I do?'

'Comply,' answered Morph. 'This guy is ninety-eight percent certain to shoot you if you try anything. Although he's unlikely to want to kill you, but you would be severely incapacitated and in extreme pain.'

'Goddamnit. I don't want this again, Morph. There must be something I can do?'

'No better options at this time.'

"I see you took out old Jackson," he gestured at the old mechanic on the floor. "Nice work," he grinned at her.

Then, in an instant, he popped off two rounds into the old guy's head. "He called me to let me know you were over here. Shame it had to end this way. I kinda liked him. Now, on the floor, face down!" This command demanded no challenge.

Dawn complied. Immediately he had one knee on her back, tying up her hands. He stepped back, took out his cellphone, and started talking in what Dawn guessed was Arabic.

*'Do you know what he's saying?'*

*'Yes, Najdi Arabic, a common dialect in Saudi Arabia. He's saying the situation has become dynamic... how long for the replacement van... too long... will improvise... leaving now.'*

He put the phone away, then went over to the old guy who was now lying in an ever-increasing pool of blood, and fished out a set of keys from a pocket. He then went around switching off lights. Once the workshop was almost in complete darkness, he grabbed Dawn by an arm and hauled her up off the floor. "Move," he said, pushing her toward the door. "And remember, don't try anything stupid."

He directed her toward a beat-up old Jeep Cherokee truck and pushed her into the back. Then he zip-tied her wrists to a secure cargo loop. Finally, he went back and closed the roller shutter door.

Dawn wondered how long it would take before the old mechanic would be found, a day, a week—who knows. Yet, clearly this guy reckoned he'd be long gone before anybody stumbled over the crime scene. He climbed into the driver's seat and looked back at her. His face was a dark shadow except for two bright white eyes. "Jackson's dead now because of you. So I'd appreciate if you don't go trying anything else. Otherwise, I'll just have to kill a few more innocent people." He put the key in the ignition and the truck rumbled into life. "You better settle in. It's gonna be a few hours before we get to where we're going."

"So where are we going?" Dawn asked.

"Oh, I'm bringing you to a bunch of people who are just dying to meet you. You got something they desperately want, and I don't intend to disappoint."

He put the truck into gear and they began to move off.

# CHAPTER 25

# NO GOING BACK

Delman read the label on the bottle of natural spring water that Madison Parker had given him and wondered what exactly were *life-force mineral compounds.* Having been robbed of his AI by that quasi-fascist, Hegarty, and his team of android agents, he had no real-time data analysis of its contents, no feedback whatsoever other than the marketing blurb on the label. For Delman, this was a singularly weird experience; like he'd been deprived of a vital sense, and now had to navigate the world from a debilitated perspective. How could he drink this if he didn't have any way to precisely measure his intake?

"It's just a bottle of water, Harry," Parker said with a slightly exasperated tone. "My understanding is, if you don't drink water, you'll die in a few days. But hey, what do I know, I'm just a human."

Delman assumed she was just being cynical, having a laugh

at his expense. Yet, without his AI to validate this response, he couldn't be sure. He snapped the cap, poured a glass, and hesitated.

"What? Do you want me to taste it for you in case it's poisoned?"

Delman frowned, then took a few tentative sips. It was the first time he had ingested anything without detailed analysis since... since, he couldn't remember, years probably. It felt very strange; he felt less than whole.

Hegarty's agents had taken his AI glasses away to forensically analyze for hacks. Yet, he suspected that it was just another way for them to weaken him so they could take over the Neuromorph Corporation under the auspices of National Security—like they did with the StarLight constellation. Now they had him on the back foot, unable to utilize his AI powers to read the room, to have proper insight on the subtext of any conversation or negotiation—to even have control over his nutritional program. It was a form of physical and psychological abuse. He would sue those vultures the first opportunity he got, all the way to the highest court in the land if necessary. He would not let them do this to him.

Dexter entered his office, stopped, and took a long hard look at him.

"What?" Delman barked, irritated by this obvious inspection.

"Man, you look like crap, Harry. Have you been eating anything?"

"I've been trying to get him to drink some water," Parker said.

"How's that going?" Dexter asked.

Delman raised his glass to each of them in turn, then took a few more sips. "Hydration in progress," he announced.

"Good, because you're going to need it. An extraordinary general meeting of the board has been scheduled for this afternoon."

Delman sighed. "That was quick."

"Yeah, well, the board has been clamoring for clarity around the security situation ever since the riot, and a swarm of government agents poking into everyone's personal tech is doing nothing to dial down the rumor mill."

"This is Hegarty's doing. The National Security Department is trying to take over, just like they did with those other tech companies. And all of their research ended up under DARPA."

"Don't be so paranoid. They have to have good reason. Nevertheless, it's time to come clean about our research over in the RainMan BioTech division. We can't keep it hidden any longer. The board needs to know."

"They'll try and use this as an opportunity to remove me as CEO. That's why they took my AI from me, Gordon. They're trying to hobble me."

"They took everyone's digital devices away for a security sweep." He opened his hands in a gesture reminiscent of someone showing they weren't armed.

"My cellphone's been taken too," Parker shook her head. "Never realized how much I need it to function. Nomophobia, they call it. Fear of being without a smartphone."

"Look, you need to face reality, Harry," Dexter said. "A move on your position as CEO is inevitable and this is their best chance to do it. Also... I've been taking the temperature among the board... and, well, they have the numbers. It's not looking good," Dexter conceded.

"Unless..." Delman stood up and came out from behind the desk. "We focus on the positives."

"Eh... those are in pretty short supply at the moment," Dexter cautioned.

"What if we don't focus on the fact that we, eh... lost our primary prototype. Instead, we put the emphasis on how it has helped us. The subject's unscheduled release into the natural environment has had the effect of accelerating the training period, leveling her up to a point that may have taken months, maybe even years. She's no longer a prototype, she's a fully realized product."

"You don't know that, Harry."

"Yeah, but neither do they," he shot back.

"The only thing they'll focus on is the fact that she's been abducted," Dexter countered. "Something that Hegarty will no doubt bring to light as he's penciled in to do the security report—first item on the agenda."

Delman thought about this for a moment. "Hegarty's as cagey as they come, so he's not going to reveal too much at the meeting, maybe just smooth over a few ruffled feathers, calm some nerves, that's all."

"Maybe, but there's always the possibility he throws a dead cat on the table," Dexter said.

"Well, we'll just have to throw one of our own. And we've got the Saudi investment deal almost across the line... even better now that they know what we're sitting on."

"Oh, and what's that, exactly?" Dexter folded his arms.

"The abduction of the prototype is a distraction," Delman waved a dismissive hand in the air. "The key point is that we have developed an extremely valuable, revolutionary technology. So we can just make another one, and another, and so on. Just think how much money we will make for the shareholders." Delman was finding his mojo returning, even without the benefit of the AI. He would not let them take him down; he would appeal to that basest of all instincts, greed. Stick with him as CEO and he would make them even richer than they already were.

~

They assembled in the boardroom on the top floor of the HQ building. Most arrived in person—those who couldn't were hooked up via a secure video conference. It took Dexter some time to call the meeting to order because there was a tense, almost fraught mood in the room. Some of the board knew the full story, some were just feeding off the rumors that National Security had taken an interest ever since the riot, some even speculated they were about to be taken over. Yet, they all knew that what was said and done at this meeting, in this room, on this afternoon, would not only determine the future course of the Neuromorph Corporation, but more importantly, the future course of their own fortunes.

Both Agent Hegarty and Agent Wisemann were there, sitting still and expressionless, waiting in the long grass ready to pounce. Delman studied Hegarty but found it impossible to gain any insight into what his intentions were. He wished he had his AI, but even it had had difficulty reading Hegarty. Perhaps that was why he was a spook, he never let his body language give away anything, and constantly deflected and misdirected with his absurd double act with Wisemann.

Yet, now that Delman was deep in the lion's den, surrounded by all these people, all shifting and jostling and talking, he felt his initial bravado beginning to slip. He couldn't read the room anymore, not without his AI. His stomach rumbled, and he realized that this was his body informing him he was hungry. Reluctantly, he fished out an organic oat, pecan, and alpine honey energy bar from a pocket, one of several that Parker had forced him to take with him, insisting that eating something was better than nothing. He didn't trust them, of course. But such was his hunger and growing discomfort that he relented and took a bite—without reading the label.

It was the most amazing thing he had ever tasted in a very, very long time. As he munched on the nutty morsel, he glanced at the ingredients list only to find it contained several on his banned list of nutrients—diglycerides, methylcellulose, palm oil, corn syrup—he almost spat it out. But... damn, it tasted good. So engrossed had he become in its scrumptiousness that he didn't even notice that Hegarty had begun delivering his report.

It was probably the phrase "Saudi investment delegation" that bumped him out of his tasting trance.

Hegarty was holding up a cellphone. "This is Jeb Marlow's phone, your Head of Security. One of several devices that were compromised during this visit to the bio-server building. This digital infection has also propagated itself throughout a number of other devices belonging to high-level executives." He then raised Delman's AI glasses. "Including that of your CEO." He cast a glance over at Delman. "This then propagated further into the core Neuromorph data stack. How deep the hack goes... we're still establishing that. However, early indications suggest that this was state-sponsored, and valuable data deemed critical to National Security has been accessed."

This admission elicited a ripple of concern around the boardroom table. There was a collective exhalation of shock.

Hegarty raised a hand to settle everyone down. "It will come as no surprise to everyone in this room just how seriously the state values the critical work being done by the Neuromorph Corporation. It is the great innovations and scientific breakthroughs that occur in this organization that help to keep our great country safe. And a lot of the credit for this must go to your CEO, Harry Delman." He swept a hand over at Delman, who was just taking another bite of his cereal bar.

"His vision and drive have propelled this organization forward, and his work with your most recent acquisition, RainMan Biotech, is worthy of a Nobel Prize."

This last statement sent a wave of confusion around the boardroom table—what work with RainMan BioTech?

"I knew they were up to something!" Rachael Rodriguez, the Director of Customer Advocacy, jabbed an accusatory finger at Delman and Dr. Matsumoto in quick succession.

"Yeah, what's been going on over there? What's our money being spent on?" shouted another director, backing up Rodriguez.

Delman was about to reply that all would be revealed once Hegarty finished with his security report, and he then had a chance to talk, but the government agent raised a hand again to get everyone's attention. "Suffice to say, it has been nothing short of revolutionary. A breakthrough of momentous proportions, and one that has been deemed so essential to the future security of our great country that it has been assigned the highest security classification—top secret."

This sparked yet another ripple of shock around the table.

"Which means, I'm sorry to say, that you will not be allowed to talk about it to anyone without sign-off from either myself or an agent within the government security apparatus with a similar or higher clearance than myself."

Delman wasn't quite sure what any of this meant. An avalanche of questions came into his mind, all hinting at some impending doom for his carefully thought-out plans.

"Let me be clear," Hegarty continued. "You will not be able to talk about it, not even to the other members of the Neuromorph board."

"What? This is outrageous," Rodriguez exclaimed. "You can't tell this board what it can and can't discuss. Who the hell do you think you are?"

"Someone, please throw this man outta here... now!" said another.

Delman almost spat out a semi-masticated glob of cereal bar. He looked over at Dexter hoping to get some clues from his reaction as to what the heck was happening here. But Dexter just sat silent, arms folded, a bemused look on his face.

Hegarty then reached into a pocket and produced a single

typewritten sheet and held it up with one hand for all to see. Even from a distance, the stylized American eagle crest of the National Security Council could be clearly seen on its masthead. "This is a directive from The National Security Council, signed by the President, ordering that the day-to-day operation of the Neuromorph Corporation, including its assets and affiliates, will now be under the sole direction of the National Security Agency."

The boardroom erupted into bedlam with several members jumping to their feet and hurling abuse at Hegarty, along with a wide range of office supplies. For Delman, it was the moment he had always feared, complete takeover by the state, using national security as its catch-all weapon. There was no going back now, no way out, no amount of clever talk and political maneuvering could undo what had just happened. He remained silent, shocked to his core, stunned into a state of suspended animation. It was the end. All that remained now was to hope that he wouldn't go slowly insane.

# CHAPTER 26
# THE DROP OFF

Yet again, Dawn found herself bound and gagged, and rolling around in the back of a moving vehicle. This time, it was the old mechanic's beat-up Jeep Cherokee. Her abductor, Malik was his name according to her AI, had given her the usual threats about making a racket before covering her over with a grimy worn tarp. It was dark outside and even darker in the back of the Jeep. She couldn't see a damn thing, and Morph was useless to her as it was just as blind as she was. If she couldn't see, then neither could the AI.

She should have run when she had the chance. With this Malik guy not wanting to injure her, he would have been cautious with his aim; she might have gotten away. But she had heeded the AI's warning—best to surrender and look for a better opportunity. Yet, her abductor would be much more cautious now, not risking any situation that might provide her with an escape option.

There was a certain irony in it, she realized. Here she was, with the most advanced AI tech on the planet embedded in her brain, and she couldn't even make a phone call. Not part of the interface design, Morph informed her. Too much power required, apparently. So as she lay there, rattling around in the back of an old Jeep, Dawn began to interrogate Morph, trying to get a better understanding of what she, and it, could and couldn't do.

Phase one of implant research at Neuromorph was the mind–machine interface. Dawn had experienced this first when communicating with external systems, in the lab, at the *Circuit Magazine* office, and with the little drone. The second phase was cognitive-augmentation; activating a built-in AI to help process data coming into her brain through either the mind–machine interface, or through her own physical senses: sight, sound, movement. But it was when she asked how all this was technically possible, that Dawn was truly shocked by the extent of biological intrusion that this tech constituted.

The problem, according to Morph, with any cranial implant was the blood–brain barrier. This was the immune system's way of preventing any foreign objects accessing brain tissue and it would begin to build up a protective layer around any wires or filaments used to send and receive signals. After a while, the subject would begin to lose the functionality of the implant.

How Neuromorph got around this problem was by utilizing the techniques it had learned in developing its bio-chips. It used the subject's own cell biology to construct the interface. In essence, the implant in Dawn's skull had been created using stem cells that had been harvested from her bone marrow. She nearly got sick when she learned of this.

As they drove on through the night, she got to asking if Morph knew anything of her background, who she was before all this happened to her. It turned out it didn't—or maybe it just wasn't saying.

Eventually, Dawn felt the Jeep turn off the highway and reduce its speed as the roads became rougher. After much turning this way and that, it finally slowed to a halt. She heard Malik get out, a crunch of gravel; muffled voices. More footsteps on gravel, and the tailgate was flung open. Bright light from a flashlight burned her eyes, and she cowered down to escape it. Strong hands grabbed her hair and turned her face to the light, then twisted it to look at the now filthy bandage on her head. More voices, speaking Mandarin.

*'What are they saying?'* she asked Morph.

*'One is a medical professional. The other is asking about your state of health.'*

She was hauled out and helped to her feet. The flashlight swept over her body, checking for injuries, as she tried to get some feeling back into her legs.

"Free her legs so she can walk." The guy with the flashlight directed this at Malik, speaking in heavily accented English.

Malik pulled out his knife and sliced the zip-ties. Then he grabbed her elbow and they started walking. As her eyes adjusted after being blinded by the flashlight, she could see they were in an old dilapidated industrial zone that was undergoing a rebuild. She cast her gaze out into the distance but couldn't see any lights anywhere. She was brought around the side of a building where a truck hauling a large shipping container was parked up. The doors of the container were open.

*'Are they putting me in there?'*

*'Yes, it looks that way,'* replied Morph.

*'There has to be a way out of here. My legs are free, maybe I could make a run for it?'* she said this as she swept her eyes around the area, hoping to give Morph something to work with.

*'You would not get far,'* Morph cautioned.

*'Maybe, but I gotta do something,'* she said.

"I need to pee," she announced to the medical guy.

He stared back at her for a second, trying to decide what to do.

"Unless you want me to mess up your nice clean shipping container," she added.

"Over there," he nodded at a beat-up old porta-potty used by the construction crew. Then he turned to Malik, inferring that he take her and make sure she didn't try to run. Malik grabbed her by the elbow and began pushing her along, letting go only when they reached the door.

Dawn gestured with her bound wrists, "If you don't mind."

Malik thought about this for a moment, then pulled out the knife again. He held it up under her chin. "Don't do anything stupid, don't make me have to shoot you." With that, he cut the zip ties on her wrists.

Dawn opened the door to the porta-potty and found it to be every bit as vile as she expected. Nevertheless, it might be a while before she had access to any sanitary facilities, so she held her nose and got on with it.

*'I should run,'* she said to Morph. *'Just burst out of here, head for the darkness and take my chances.'*

*'Unwise. Your chances of escape would be less than 2%.'*

Before Dawn could argue, she overheard whispered voices but too low and hushed to make out the conversation. *'Do you hear that, Morph?'*

*'Yes. Malik is arguing with the medic. Would you like me to amplify?'*

*'Absolutely. What are they saying?'* Suddenly the amplitude of the whispered conversation grew louder in her head and she began to make out sentences.

"This was not the deal," Malik whispered. "I've brought her here. My part in this is over."

"No. The deal was to bring her to a drop-off yet to be determined. And it has now been determined that that location is the mainland. You are to accompany the subject on board the ship."

"What? To China?" Malik's voice grew even louder.

"Deliver the subject as agreed. Then the contract is complete," the medic insisted.

"This is bullshit. Why do I need to do this?"

There was a moment's silence before the medic spoke again. "Listen, we need you on the ship. The crew are just merchant sailors, not trained operatives, they've simply been commandeered. Anyway, you need a way out, so this is it. Guard her on the journey and then you're done."

There was no reply. Perhaps Malik had accepted his fate.

*'They're shipping me to China, Morph.'* Dawn felt her escape

opportunities slipping away. It was now or never. She pulled herself together and psyched herself up to make a run for it.

But the door suddenly burst open and Malik grabbed her before she could think. He dragged her out, the medic came over, and she felt a pinprick in her shoulder. She looked around in shock to see him emptying the contents of a syringe into her bloodstream. Almost immediately, she felt her legs give out, the darkness grew around her, and she slipped into unconsciousness.

# CHAPTER 27
# ENTOMBED

Dawn awoke this time to complete darkness. Thinking she might have gone blind, she blinked several times, yet she couldn't make out any discernible features in the total blackness. She shifted her body, expecting to still be bound with zip ties, only to discover that she was now strapped down to some type of gurney. She could feel the thin mattress beneath her and the thick straps that held her arms and legs down tight. She could also feel the edges of an oxygen mask fitted over her nose and mouth.

'Morph?' she asked.

'Yes, Dawn. I am here,' it replied.

'Where am I?'

'Good question,' Morph replied. 'Could you say hello out loud?'

'Are you serious?'

'Yes.'

*'Okay.'* It seemed like a weird request but what the heck, she said "hello" out loud.

Her voice was dull and muffled. A consequence of the oxygen mask, she assumed.

*'Even accounting for the mask covering your mouth, my analysis suggests that you're in an enclosed space with a considerable amount of sound-absorbing material surrounding you. Given that our last known location was entering the back of a shipping container, my best guess is that you're still in the container, surrounded by packing crates designed to minimize any sound you might make, or perhaps to shield you from a possible customs inspection X-ray machine.'*

"Dammit, there must be a way out of here," she muttered, as she began rattling the gurney, pulling on her legs and arms in the hope that something might give. She shook and raged, trying over and over to break something, but nothing gave way. In the end, Dawn laid back, exhausted.

*'I should have run when I had the chance, Morph. Now there's no getting out of here. They're putting me on a ship, bringing me to China, I guess.'*

*'That would also be my assessment of the situation,'* said the AI.

There was a sudden clunk, and the entire shipping container began moving up and swinging around. Dawn felt like she was on a roller coaster being pitched this way and that. A moment later, it dropped down again, followed by another clunk, no doubt settling into position on top of the stack of other containers. This was followed by a series of more clunks on top of her and to the sides.

*'Oh my God, they're not going to bury me in here, are they?'*

*'Unlikely,'* replied Morph. *'Remember, you are an extremely*

valuable asset, and they will want to keep you alive for as long as possible to examine you.'

'Thanks,' Dawn said, 'but that's not very comforting. Being buried alive or being a lab rat... it's not much of a choice, is it?'

'I detect a note of pessimism in your voice, Dawn. We must not give up hope that there will be a satisfactory conclusion to this adventure.'

'Do me a favor, Morph, shut up and let me be miserable in peace.'

Nothing more happened for quite some time, leaving Dawn alone with her thoughts of a long, slow death inside a shipping container. Eventually though, she heard the mighty ship's engines start to power up, and the vessel began to move, sideways at first, then slowly maneuvering to depart from the port. She could feel the change in the rocking motion of the ship as it left the calm waters of the port and entered the choppier waters of the open ocean. With the drone of the engines and the rocking and rolling of the ship, Dawn found herself drifting off to sleep again, only to be abruptly jolted back to reality by the sound of the container doors being flung open.

Dim light entered, enough for her to make out the shapes of the cardboard packing crates all around her. She heard voices speaking Mandarin and the shifting, shuffling sounds of crates being removed as they dug their way toward her. She felt like some ancient Egyptian princess, entombed in her pyramid as the raiders dismantled it block by block, inching ever closer toward their prize. A burst of sunlight flooded in as the wall of packing crates began to be disassembled. There were several of them working in a chain, clearing the path until finally, they stepped aside to allow three other people to gain access to her. One swiftly checked her over and they began to wheel the gurney out of the container, which had been positioned in a vast stack of other containers so that it could be easily accessed from a walkway. As her eyes adjusted to the light, Dawn could see a cliff-like wall of containers stacked high all around her.

They brought her into the working area of the ship, through long corridors, until she finally came to rest in what looked like the ship's medical bay. Another man entered, dressed in a crisp, white shirt and trousers of a quasi-naval uniform. Dawn took him to be the ship's captain. He gestured to one of the medics, who reached over and removed the oxygen mask from Dawn's face. She was tempted to hurl a stream of abuse at them, but reconsidered. It might be best if she seemed more compliant, less of a threat. Maybe that way she could find an opportunity to locate a signal source and get a message out.

The captain spoke. "Please be aware that our instructions are to ensure your safety and comfort during this trip. You will be given a cabin, clean clothes, food, and a place to freshen up. However, this is dependent on your complete cooperation. Any indication or action that we deem to be disobedient or disagreeable will result in your incarceration down in the hold instead of comfortable accommodation. I am now going to instruct that you be released from these bonds. But first, I need you to tell me that you understand our agreement and that you will not try to undermine it. Please bear in mind that you are now on a container ship far out to sea. There is no way off this ship, so there's no point in trying to escape as this is not possible. Do we have an agreement?"

"Yes, fine," Dawn said. "Now untie me and let me stretch my muscles."

There was a moment's hesitation by the captain, as if he was considering that she wasn't being fully sincere with him. However, he conceded, nodding to a medic, who proceeded to unfasten the straps that bound her to the gurney.

She sat up, tried to rub some feeling back into her arms, and forced down a burning desire to vent her anger and frustration at these people. But she needed to give them the sense that she wasn't going to be a problem. She also knew that these guys were not part of any state-sponsored security agency, just simply sailors who had been commandeered into delivering her safely to wherever the hell it was they were ultimately taking her.

A short while later, after they had given her yet another medical examination, along with some food and water, they escorted her out of the medical bay, telling her that they were bringing her to a cabin where she could be more comfortable. It involved more long corridors and elevators, but in one area, she felt her head start tingling again. It grew stronger and stronger as she passed a certain point in the ship. This, she assumed, must be the epicenter of the onboard data network. She tried desperately to focus on the signal and began to differentiate various subsystems, but once they passed through yet another steel bulkhead and the door closed behind her, the signal was all but lost.

'Dammit,' she said to Morph in her mind, 'I almost made a connection there, now it's gone.'

'Yes, I sensed it too,' Morph replied. 'Unfortunately, the steel structure of the ship acts as a significant barrier for RF signals.'

She was ushered into a small, compact cabin—clean, but utilitarian. The walls were bare but at least there was a window looking out to sea. On a small table was a tray of food, water, and some toiletries. On the bed, a set of the ship's company overalls were laid out.

"This will be your cabin for the duration of the trip. There are sanitary facilities through that door. Please make yourself as comfortable as possible," said the captain. He then gave her a curt nod and left the cabin. She heard the door lock behind him.

Dawn sat down on the edge of the bunk and considered her situation. She was moving further and further away from land with each passing hour. Her only hope now was to try and get out of this cabin somehow, then see if she could hone in on that data signal again. That way, she might be able to send a message before it was too late... which she was beginning to think it probably was.

# CHAPTER 28
# LIFE'S FUNNY

Delman heard footsteps approaching along the corridor toward the master suite onboard his luxury superyacht, Saffron. He reckoned it was probably his long-suffering Chief Steward, Maria-Luisa Santos, making yet another attempt to have the suite cleaned. But the footfall sounded heavier and the knock on the door more assertive.

"Harry? Are you in there?" It was Dexter.

*Who the heck let him on board?* Delman wondered. He groaned and pulled the duvet over his head.

The door opened. "Harry? It's Gordon. I'm just here to see if you're okay."

Delman didn't answer; instead, he just tried to bury his head further into the pillow.

He heard Dexter's footsteps entering the bedroom.

"Harry, what the hell. Are you hiding under the duvet?"

"Go away," was Delman's muffled response.

"Jeez, Harry, you need to get a grip."

Delman pulled back the duvet from his face and sat up a little. "What for? They've taken everything away from me."

Dexter stood, hands on hips, shaking his head at the sad and sorry state of his business partner. After Agent Hegarty dropped the bombshell at the EGM, the lawyers immediately moved in and began explaining to everyone how the takeover was going to work—what they could and couldn't do, what they could and couldn't say, all under the auspices of that catchall directive that allowed the government to do whatever the heck they liked: national security. Delman couldn't bear it. So he left the meeting, headed back to his yacht, and ordered a high-fat, high-carb, highly satisfying takeout from a local Italian diner and washed it down with half a bottle of Sonoma Coast Pinot Noir. After that, he crashed, and he had not gotten up since, except to go to the toilet and open his cabin door to all the subsequent takeouts he had ordered since.

Dexter moved over to the wide window that that opened onto the deck of the yacht's master cabin and pulled back the curtain just a little, to let some daylight in. Delman shielded his eyes from the blast of sun that shafted through the gap. Dexter then surveyed the mess of food cartons, plates, utensils, bottles, and cans that were strewn all over every flat surface. Then to the piles of clothing that had been dumped in a heap on the floor. Finally, he looked back at Delman with a patronly, slightly exasperated expression. He gave a long slow sigh. "How long is this going to go on for, Harry?"

Delman sat up and hung his head. "I don't see the point anymore."

"The point is you're still CEO of the most valuable biotech company on the planet. Sure, the machinery of the state has moved in to protect what they see as a national security asset. But it's still business as usual, Harry. Better yet, we can develop our AI-enhanced neural implant without worrying about the legal gray areas we were currently operating under. We also get access to all of the other top-secret developments going on under DARPA, as well as access to some of the best scientific brains in the business. So, you need to start seeing the upside here."

Dexter had clearly adapted to the new regime in record time; maybe they had made him an offer he couldn't refuse. Yet, Delman could only see what he had lost, and that was control of the vision. It was out of his hands now, he would have to run everything by a committee to get anything done and that's not how he liked to work; he would not be answerable to anyone.

"Have they found her yet?" he asked.

Dexter cleared a space for himself to sit down. "Not yet. And we should not exclude the possibility that she's dead."

"Have they any clues, leads... anything to go on?"

"I don't know. Hegarty and his team are being tight-lipped about the ongoing investigation," Dexter said. "But I did learn that the Saudis were also being played."

"What do you mean?" Delman sat up in shock at this revelation. "That was a solid deal, we had the money in escrow."

Dexter shook his head. "The money was Chinese, and the escrow account was fake. Prince Waleed had been so desperate to get back in the good books with the regime that he fell for a scam. He looks to be a genuine investor but the financial backing he had put in place was all smoke and mirrors, set up by our Asian friends to facilitate a major hack on the bio-server. The security guy, Malik, was working as a double agent. The whole operation was blown when Dawn Harrison did a runner. They abandoned it to capture her. She has everything they want, literally inside her head. To be honest, we might never have known we were being hacked otherwise. That's what got the NSA guys so spooked. Apparently, the Saudi deal was already under investigation by the CFIUS."

Strangely, Delman's initial shocked reaction to this news faded almost instantly. He considered that he should feel something, loss, betrayal... anger. But there was nothing, he just didn't care anymore. All that remained was a great big void that was being filled with copious amounts of apathy, ennui, and takeouts.

Delman grunted. "Life's funny, isn't it." He looked up. "Don't you think life's funny, Gordon?"

Dexter gave him a curious look. "Yeah, sure," he nodded sympathetically, with just a hint of pity in his voice. He stood up and glanced around at the messy room again. "I'm going to get Parker to organize a cleanup of this place."

"No, I don't want to see anyone. And I'm perfectly capable of looking after myself."

"Okay. But you need to snap out of this, Harry. I'll check back tomorrow. In the meantime, here's something for you." He reached into a pocket and pulled out a small box. He offered it to Delman.

"What is it?"

"Your new AI glasses. I had the techs over in development put together a new set."

Delman shook his head. "I don't need them. Not anymore."

Dexter gave him a hard look. "Yes, you do. Remember what happened last time you went without them?"

"I said, I don't need them."

Dexter sighed, a resigned expression on his face. "Fine. I'll leave them here in case you change your mind." He placed them carefully on the bedside locker, then got up and headed out of the suite.

# CHAPTER 29
# THE TEST

Dawn stepped into the tiny cabin shower and stood for a moment just letting the water massage her aching muscles. She could feel the tension in her body wash away along with all the accumulated dirt and grime of the last few days. She rubbed a hand over her head; her hair was beginning to grow again. Her skull was no longer the smooth fleshy egg it had once been. Now it had a fuzzy, velvety feel. She fingered the bandage, its edges were beginning to break free from her scalp, and it was intensely itchy, probably from all the hair now trying to break out into the open.

She took her time washing and then drying herself with a rough, but clean towel. Finally, she looked at her face in the small mirror above a stainless steel sink and examined the bandage. She was severely tempted to just rip it off in one quick bite of pain. But not knowing what lay beneath, she thought the better of this strategy. Instead, she slowly peeled at the edges, millimeter by millimeter, until it finally came away.

Leaning in and examining the scar, she was surprised to find it was just a straight line no bigger than the width of her thumb, and it had healed nicely. She then spent a few satisfying moments scratching the area all around it.

There was a noticeable change in the low rumble of the ship's engine; it was speeding up. She glanced out the small window and calculated their speed at eighteen knots. How did she know this? She also knew that this was a Post-Panamax class container ship, transporting around seven thousand containers and bound for Guangzhou Port, in the People's Republic of China. How did she suddenly know all this?

'Morph?'

'Yes, Dawn.'

'What's going on? I seem to know things that I shouldn't possibly know.'

'The third phase of neural assimilation is advancing, where my knowledge base and logic reasoning becomes subsumed into your subconscious, and communication is no longer the cumbersome call and response. It's simply executed by thought alone.'

'You're joking me?'

'No, I'm not. This is a very exciting moment. This symbiosis of mind and machine was only ever considered theoretical. Even those who designed your neural implant were not completely convinced that it was possible. But it seems your brain has fully adapted to the cognitive augmentation.'

Dawn felt a little overwhelmed; her head spun and she had to grip the edge of the sink to steady herself.

*'This is incredible,'* she said, as she moved over to the small bunk and sat down, trying to take it all in. But her mind wouldn't settle. It kept coming back to her increasing desire to get off this ship, somehow... before it got too far away from land. With her new-found abilities, she began to calculate the distance. If it departed from the port of Los Angeles and traveled at an average of eighteen knots per hour, then... it was already entering international waters—the high seas. The US Coast Guard would have no jurisdiction out here. Boarding a foreign container ship would cause a huge diplomatic incident. Would they risk that for her? Possibly, but the odds weren't good, considering they probably didn't even know where she was.

Dawn stood up and got dressed in ship's overalls and jacket. Then banged on the door.

"Hey, any chance of getting some fresh air? I'm going to throw up in here."

She had to bang a few more times before someone took notice. The lock turned, the door opened, and she stepped back when she saw that it was Malik standing on the other side.

"If you want some air, come, now," he barked at her, his face a mask of contempt.

She stood for a moment trying to figure out what insult she could fire back at him. "So they wouldn't let you go either. Or maybe you just like my company?"

His face twitched, as if he were holding himself back from striking her for such insolence. But Dawn had already calculated the probable thrust of an attack and had worked through a series of moves to counter it, slip past, and lock him in the cabin. All this she had figured out in the instant it had taken her to consider it. It gave her a boost to her bravado, yet she best not push her luck too much.

She walked out past him, and could feel the tension knotting him up. "You'd better lead the way," she gestured, with a smile, almost taunting him.

He jabbed a finger at her. "Remember, we're on a ship in the middle of the Pacific; there's no way off—just in case you're thinking of trying something."

"No need to tie me up and gag me, then. Or do you just do that for fun?" she taunted him. He was desperately trying to keep control, trying not to lash out. They wanted her whole, healthy, and uninjured—and it was killing him inside.

"Let's go," he ordered.

They descended a level and out a starboard doorway onto a long narrow, covered deck that ran all the way from the stern of the ship to the bow. Behind her, a wall of stacked shipping containers towered overhead. The air was fresh and salty. Dawn took a few deep reinvigorating breaths. Then she reoriented herself to where she had detected the RF signals when she first arrived on the ship. She made her way toward the bridge located near the stern; the tingling in her head grew more intense. But unlike before, she could instantly discern a multitude of distinct frequencies and patterns. She rested her arms on the railing, looking out to sea, and focused all her attention on the signals.

"We go back now," Malik announced. He didn't look comfortable out here, it was not his natural environment. He gripped his jacket with one hand at the neck, his arms squeezed tight into his body.

"Just a few more minutes. I'm still feeling nauseous, a bit more fresh air and I'll be fine."

He grunted, but didn't protest.

Dawn refocused her attention. The signal began to tessellate into distinct patterns, yet one stood out from all the others. As she honed in on it, she realized it was another AI, one that managed all the ship's systems. But this AI also noticed her in the data stream and questioned her presence, asking who she was and what she wanted. Dawn ran through a multitude of possible responses, eventually deciding to act as a test protocol and informed the AI that she was here to evaluate its performance and make recommendations on whether it should be decommissioned and replaced with a different version. The ship's AI replied that it would consider it an honor to be evaluated.

A ripple of anxious excitement shot through Dawn's body at the thought that she might finally have a way out. She calmed herself down, not wishing to blow it by losing her concentration. She focused on this new AI connection, interrogating it, seeking out a comms link to the outside world, and tracked it to the Inmarsat global maritime communications satellite system, to which the AI was connected and could utilize.

She had done it. She'd finally found a way. Now, the only question in her mind was, who to call?

"It's time, let's go." Malik grabbed her arm and pulled.

But in one swift movement, without even thinking about it,

Dawn clasped her hands together and bent her elbow and pulled out of his grip. She stepped back and to the side, adopting a defensive stance, ready for the next move.

Malik hesitated, reevaluating her. He had not considered that she might know some fancy footwork, she might even have had training in the martial arts. This was also a shock to Dawn, as she had no prior knowledge of these moves; they seemed to come out of nowhere.

She raised a hand in a gesture of appeasement as she badly needed more time to get a message out. "Look, we're both going to be on this ship together for a few weeks, so I suggest you go take a chill pill. Unless of course you want to go for that gun that you keep at the base of your spine and put a bullet in my head. But I don't think your paymasters would let you live very long after that, would they?"

She could see the anger in him start to dial up. Maybe he just didn't like women, or women that fought back—or maybe he just didn't like being stuck on this boat for the next few weeks playing chaperone to someone he couldn't beat up.

"Two minutes," he jerked a pair of fingers at her. "Then we go back. I'm freezing out here." He pulled his suit jacket tighter and shuffled off into the protection of a sheltered alcove to wait.

Dawn wasted no time reestablishing the data connection via the ship's AI, with the Inmarsat constellation. Without considering it, she found herself attempting to establish a connection with the primary AI back in the Neuromorph HQ. Why this AI? She did not know. Perhaps it was Morph directing her from the neural shadows. But it was a good choice because as soon as the connection was made, a stream of data began to be exchanged.

Dawn learned of the NSA's involvement in the corporation's affairs, the frantic hunt to find her, and the hacking attempt by the Chinese using a Saudi prince as a proxy. At the same time as this information was streaming into her brain, she was sending everything she knew about her location, the ship she was on, and her understanding of where they were taking her. Lastly, she gave an instruction to the Neuromorph AI to inform whoever was best placed to effect her rescue, because she had made up her mind—she was getting off this ship tonight, one way or another.

"Time," Malik shouted over from his alcove.

With the data transfer completed, she turned and began to head back to her cabin, the connection fading as she went. Yet, before it died completely, she sensed the ship's AI wondering if it had passed the test. Dawn informed it that the first test had been successful, meeting all requirements. But there would be more to come, the evaluation was not over just yet. The AI replied that it was one hundred percent ready for all further tests, and was confident that it would perform to a level beyond her satisfaction.

# CHAPTER 30
# GUT FEELING

'I would strongly advise you against this course of action.' Morph's voice resonated inside Dawn's head.

'Fine. But I'm still doing it. I'm not staying on this ship any longer than I have to.'

'My advice is to wait until there is a better opportunity for escape, one that does not involve potential death by hypothermia in the Pacific Ocean.'

'There are no perfect opportunities, Morph. I should have run when I had the chance back at that airfield, but no, I listened to you, and now look where I am... half-way around the world.'

'You are not half-way around the world,' it corrected her. 'Only three hundred and eighty-nine nautical miles from the California coast, which I should remind you is much further than the range of this ship's lifeboat.'

'Well, every now and again you just gotta go with your gut. And my gut tells me that getting off this ship right now is a much better idea than staying on it while it takes me to be someone else's experiment.'

'Very well, you do seem very determined to continue with this reckless course of action.'

'Damn right I am.'

She checked the hour on her internal clock, 1:30 AM. 'Okay, Morph. Time to saddle up.'

Earlier that evening, Dawn had combed every inch of her cabin to find a suitable implement to jimmy open the door. She found a short, flat steel bar as part of the bed support, and with some tugging and pulling was able to free it. She gripped it with both hands and jammed the flat end into the gap between the door lock and the surround, leaned on it a few times, pushing it this way and that, and eventually created a gap for the lock bolt to pass through.

She opened the door, taking a peek left and right down the dimly lit corridor, then stepped out, keeping a tight grip on the bar as a weapon. Her plan of escape involved several carefully considered steps, all of which went to crap as soon as she turned the first corner. A startled crew member stood there holding a drink in one hand and a half-eaten roll in the other, presumably he had just come off shift and was heading back to his cabin. They eyed each other for a moment, not knowing quite what to do. Dawn could see the wheels in his brain start to spin, he was going to run. Sure enough, he dropped his supper and made a dash for it. But she was on him in an instant, sweeping out a leg to trip him up. He went sprawling, front first on the floor. However, he was quick to pick himself up, rolling over and trying to claw his way back up onto his feet.

Dawn swiveled a kick to the side of his head and caught him hard, sending him bouncing off the side wall. He dropped to the floor, and didn't move.

*'Goddammit, I hope I haven't killed him,'* she thought, eying the stricken sailor.

*'I told you this was a bad plan,'* the AI said.

*'You're not much help at the moment, Morph are you?'*

*'Just saying.'*

Dawn knelt down over the inert body. He was still breathing, she relaxed a little. He was out cold, nothing more.

*'Now what?'* she wondered.

*'You could throw him over the side of the ship. It would be a long time before he's found, if ever,'* Morph offered.

*'Are you serious? That's a bit dark.'*

*'Alternatively, you could drag him all the way back to your cabin and tie him up.'*

Dawn reached down and grabbed him by the ankles and began hauling him to the cabin. Then she tied him to a metal support and checked he was okay.

*'He could come around at any time and begin yelling,'* Morph warned.

*'Good point,'* she conceded, and stuffed a gag into his mouth, making sure he could still breathe. Then headed out of the cabin again. This was a bad start to her escape plan.

She made her way to the starboard walkway without further incident and exited out through a thick steel door to be greeted by a fresh night-time breeze. The sea was a cold black expanse, flecked with white-tipped rolling waves, and illuminated by the light of a full moon. She shivered a little, zipped up her jacket, and began making her way to where she could connect with the ship's AI.

She concealed herself in the same secluded alcove where Malik had sought shelter earlier that day, and began to interrogate the ship's systems, seeking out the information she was going to need. After a few moments, she knew where everything that mattered was located, including the locations of all crew, how many were currently on the bridge, the location of the lifeboat, and which walkways and corridors had CCTV operating—these she would avoid. Lastly, she thanked the AI for its help but informed it that the evaluation wasn't over just yet.

Her plan was to take the free-fall lifeboat that hung precipitously over the stern of the giant container ship, but before she could do that, there was equipment she needed that would give her a fighting chance of surviving the unforgiving Pacific Ocean. She left the shelter of the alcove and began making her way toward a locker room further along the walkway.

A moment or two later, she was inside grabbing a bag with a rolled-up immersion suit. If she were to fall into the water out here, she wouldn't last long before succumbing to hypothermia and drowning. This suit would give her more time. The next thing she looked for was a "grab bag," which should contain additional survival equipment already packed and ready to take in a hurry. She took out the first one she saw, opened it up, and began rummaging through it until she found what she was looking for. A small handheld device that looked very similar to a VHF radio, except this was a sat-phone that used the Inmarsat constellation. Morph had assured her that she would be able to connect directly to the primary AI at the Neuromorph HQ, just as she had with the ship's AI. She stuffed it into the bag without checking it, along with the immersion suit, a jack knife and a flashlight. She slung the bag over her shoulder and headed out of the locker room to execute the next element of her plan.

Outside, the clouds had closed in, obscuring the light of the moon. This suited her as she felt a little less exposed on the connecting walkway that brought her over to the port side of the ship where the fast-rescue craft was located—an open-topped rigid inflatable with two powerful outboard engines. Dawn had considered using this as her escape vehicle but it had a very limited range, being primarily used for man-overboard search and rescue or ship maintenance. It was also open to the elements and Dawn didn't fancy bobbing around in an angry sea with no fuel and no shelter.

She halted for a moment to focus her mind back on the ship's systems, checking the location of the crew and any exposure she might have to a CCTV camera. Sure enough, one was pointing in a direction that covered the rescue craft. She instructed the AI to freeze the frame. It obliged. She then instructed it to shut down the ship's engines, fifteen minutes from now. That should be more than enough time, she reckoned.

She clambered onboard, unfolded the blade of the jack knife, and cut the fuel line. Next, she found the fuel tank and punched several holes in it. By the time they realized she was gone and piled into the rescue craft to go after her, it would be completely drained of fuel.

Yet, just to be sure, she clambered back out onto the deck and worked the release lever. The boat dropped down the side of the ship entering the water with a splash. She looked over the railing, expecting to see it disappear off into the darkness, but it was still attached by a single rope line.

*'Dammit, I thought this was supposed to just float free.'*

*'Perhaps it's an additional safety measure not mentioned in the manual,'* said Morph.

*'Now what?'* she said.

*'That's a good question.'*

The rescue boat bounced along the water, banging against the hull of the ship. Someone was going to notice the thumping sound and begin to investigate. Dawn frantically followed the rope line to a point on the rigging that was just within reach. She took out the jack knife and started cutting the thick rope.

A deck light flicked on further down the walkway.

*'Crap, someone's coming to check,'* she said.

*'I would advise getting out of here and to your ultimate destination as fast as you can.'*

Dawn kept hacking at the rope. A side door opened and someone stepped out on deck just as the rope severed and the rescue boat floated free.

She had no more time to waste, if she wanted to get off this ship then it was now or never. She ran back across the connecting walkway and then made a beeline for the stern. She bounded up the metal staircase that led to the gantry for the free-fall lifeboat, situated behind the bridge. As she came around a corner to access the gantry, two crew had already come out from the bridge, probably having just been alerted that the rescue craft had launched.

There was no time to think. Dawn ran straight at them, hoping that the element of surprise would be to her advantage. She shouldered one out of the way, but the other made a grab for her, catching a strap on her bag. She swung around, pulling him toward her and kneed him in the abdomen. He let go of the bag and crumpled on the deck.

Dawn leaped onto the stern of the lifeboat. It hung down almost vertically on a slide and it was the ship's only lifeboat. With it gone, and the rescue boat jettisoned, there would be no way to catch her. She opened the hatch and found her way into the coxswain seat, shutting the hatch behind her. She strapped herself into the harness, good and tight. It was designed to accommodate thirty people, but because it now had only one occupant there was a high likelihood it would bounce and flip over when it hit the water. Yet it should right itself after the initial impact, she hoped. Dawn could hear shouts from outside the hatch. It was now or never. She gripped the lever on the side of her seat and pumped it several times to release the boat.

It dropped, and for a second or two she was in free fall before being slammed forward as the boat impacted the water... then kept going down. Dawn could see the water rise up over the port holes and for a brief moment it was completely submerged. Then it shot back out of the water, becoming briefly airborne and did a complete bow over stern flip, smacking down on the water again. It rocked back and forth for a moment before finally righting itself in the water.

Dawn hit the start button and the engine sputtered into life.

She put it into gear and the boat began to move. As it did, she turned the wheel to face east, then pushed the throttle all the way forward, and breathed a sigh of relief. The lifeboat would now chug along at a steady six knots for the next twenty-four hours or so. Not enough to reach the coast, not even enough to make it back into US coastal waters. But it was enough for now. She would worry about all that later... when the fuel ran out.

# CHAPTER 31
## SEA LIONS

Harry Delman stood stark naked on the deck outside the master suite of his luxury superyacht, his thin frame silhouetted against the backdrop of San Francisco Bay. The early sun warmed his body, the salt-laden air feathered his bare skin, and each new breath filled his nostrils with the scent of the sea. He closed his eyes, drawing in another breath. This one deeper, more intentional. He felt the air fill every corner of his lungs, imagining it purging the stale thoughts and weighty responsibilities that had clouded his mind. As he exhaled, the breath escaped his lips in a slow, controlled stream, carrying with it the burdens of his role as a visionary genius and potential savior of human civilization.

Above him, a flock of seagulls dotted the sky, their white wings catching the sunlight as they dove and squabbled over morsels of food unseen by the human eye, their raucous cries piercing the air. Their movements a ballet of instinct, almost as old as time itself.

Across the gently lapping waters, a colony of sea lions had claimed a weathered pontoon as an unlikely oasis. Lounging on its sun-bleached planks, their sleek bodies glistened in the golden warmth that bathed both man and beast alike. Some slipped into the water with fluid grace, barely disturbing the surface as they vanished into the depths. Others rolled onto their backs, exposing pale bellies to the sun. Their flippers moved with endearing determination as they scratched and shifted, finding comfort on their sunlit sanctuary.

Delman stood transfixed, marveling at the sight before him. How had he missed this spectacle for so long? His yacht had been berthed here for months, yet only now did he truly see all this life teeming around him. Each movement, each sound, each smell now seemed to him a revelation. The world, once muted and distant, had suddenly burst into vibrant life.

In this moment of clarity, he realized he was no longer a mere observer but a part of this living, breathing tapestry. The boundary between his world and the natural world had dissolved, leaving him awash in a newfound sense of connection and wonder.

It was a primordial elixir, awakening long-dormant evolutionary senses within him. He was simply a man, wrought from flesh and bone standing at the edge of land and sea, rediscovering the profound simplicity of existence.

For the first time in many, many years, without the distortion filter of his AI, he was seeing the world for what it is. He could feel it, hear it, smell it... and it was glorious.

"Mr. Delman?"

He turned around to find Maria-Luisa standing behind him waving a cellphone. She shrieked and turned her head away when she realized he was naked.

Delman frantically went to cover his private parts with his hands, only to stop and consider that the sea lions don't have to do this every time they meet each other. So he simply stood there, arms akimbo.

"It's Mr. Dexter." Maria-Luisa waved the cellphone again, averting her gaze. "He wants to speak to you, says it's very important. I said I can't disturb you, I'd get fired if I disturb Mr. Delman. He said he'd give me ten thousand dollars if I get you on the phone. I said I'd try." She jiggled the phone again.

Delman sighed, reached out and took it from her. "It's okay, thank you."

Maria-Luisa scurried out of the suite.

"Hello, Gordon. How are you today? I've just been watching the sea lions. I think I would like to be a sea lion."

"Jeez, Harry. I've been trying to contact you for the last hour or more. Where are the new AI glasses I left with you? Why aren't you wearing them?"

"I don't need them anymore. I'm seeing the world for what it is now. I was blind, but now my eyes are open."

"Harry, are you okay?"

"Never better. I've been giving a lot of thought to what we've been doing, Gordon. About our rush to merge mind and machine. And I'm beginning to think that it might not be such a good idea."

"What? Listen, Harry, I understand losing control of

Neuromorph has hit you hard, but you just need some rest and you'll be back in the saddle in no time."

"You don't understand, Gordon. Without my AI glasses, I'm now thinking for myself for the first time in years."

"Yeah, whatever. Listen—are you ready for this?"

"What?"

"She's made contact. Dawn Harrison is still alive."

"Alive?" Harry almost dropped the phone. "How? When?"

"We got a data dump on the Neuromorph AI around a few hours ago. It seems she's on a Chinese container ship, somewhere out in the Pacific, bound for Guangzhou. And... get this... she hacked into the ship's own AI and instigated a data transfer using the Inmarsat constellation. Incredible."

Delman stood motionless trying to process this revelation. Not only was Dawn Harrison still alive, but it seemed like she'd leveled up her cognitive abilities far beyond anything he had ever imagined. Thoughts of sea lions and seagulls, and his doubts about the ethics of AI, suddenly vanished from his mind. "Can we communicate with her?"

"Not in real-time. But if she reconnects with the Neuromorph AI again, we can leave a message for her. However, we think she's planning an escape."

"An escape? How?"

"We don't know as yet. But she's getting off somehow. Hegarty's now pulling out all the stops to get to that ship as fast as possible. And that's where you come in."

"Sure, how?"

"He wants to commandeer your yacht."

"What?" Delman did not expect this. "No way. They've

already taken everything from me, now they want my home too?"

"Hey, you've got no choice in this, Harry. They're already on their way."

"Who?"

"Christ, Harry. Who do you think? Hegarty and his team of cyborgs."

"They're not taking over my yacht. I won't let them."

"You do want to find her, don't you?" Dexter's tone was calm but firm.

"Eh, yes, of course I do."

"Then they need your vessel, it's the fastest ship available. The Chinese container ship is a couple of hundred nautical miles off the west coast. Too far for a rescue helicopter. They've already dispatched a US Coast Guard fast response cutter from San Pedro, but it only has a top speed of twenty-five knots. Yours does at least sixty, so I've been told. And it's fully integrated with the Neuromorph AI so they can also coordinate the entire operation from your ship."

Delman sighed, he could see the logic in this action, his was one of the fastest superyachts in the world. "Okay, fine. I suppose I'd better get dressed then."

∼

Delman got dressed in a pair of hastily donned sweatpants with a zip-up hoodie over a food-stained t-shirt depicting a circuit diagram with the slogan *resistance is futile*. He ventured out of the master suite of his superyacht for the first time in what seemed to him like an eternity. By the time he got to the port side walkway, he could see several black SUVs already pulling up on the dock. Dark-suited NSA goons started spilled out of the vehicles and began unloading boxes and crates of equipment.

He spotted Madison Parker coming up the gangplank along with Gordon Dexter and Jeb Marlow close behind. She gave him a cheery wave. Delman reckoned they had been sent in the vanguard to try and placate him, keep his frustration at this intrusion from boiling over.

"Harry," she said, a bright smile on her face. "You're vertical I see."

Delman huffed, and kept his gaze fixed on the activities taking place along the dock. Three tanker trucks had just rolled up, ready to begin the process of bunkering thirty thousand liters of fuel.

"You're not wearing your AI glasses?"

"No," Delman shook his head. "I'm going organic."

Furtive glances were exchanged between Parker, Dexter, and Marlow. "You still have them? You didn't throw them away or anything?" she asked.

"Yes, of course I do," Delman said. "What do you take me for? They're still on the bedside locker where Gordon left them."

"It's just, remember what happened the last time you went without them?" Parker cautioned. "It took a while for you to stabilize after that episode."

"Hey, you're supposed to be my personal assistant, not my

nanny. I tell you what to do, not the other way around. That's the way it works," Delman snapped back at her.

"Of course, Harry. We're just... concerned, is all," Dexter said.

"What I'm concerned about is all this crap." Delman swept a hand over the dockside, which was now a hive of NSA activity.

Again, more furtive glances before Marlow spoke. "The NSA people are setting up in the main salon. Fuel bunkering will take approximately forty minutes, so they plan to be up and running by then."

Delman spotted Agents Hegarty and Wisemann deep in discussion at the foot of the gangplank. No doubt plotting some further injury to his privacy. "Okay, whatever," he said with a sigh. "I'm going back to my suite until we're ready to set sail. Make sure nobody, and I mean nobody, disturbs me."

"Of course, good idea," Parker said, smiling broadly.

Delman grunted and headed back to his sanctuary.

Forty-five minutes later, the ship was powering up its engines, throwing off its mooring lines, and began nosing its way out of Clipper Cove. The Captain turned its bow west and aimed for the open sea. After another ten minutes, it was passing under the Golden Gate Bridge, and twenty minutes after that, as it entered the main shipping lanes, the Captain opened it up. The bow rose out of the water as the powerful Paxman 18-Cylinder engines sucked in gargantuan quantities of fuel, pushing the craft through the water at a bone-slapping sixty knots.

# CHAPTER 32
# EMERGENCY

M alik Al-Sayf felt a noticeable change in the tone of the ship's engines, and even though he was not familiar with the workings of ocean-going container ships, he had been on enough Saudi superyachts in his time to know that something significant was happening. The ship was slowing down, coming to a halt, something that it shouldn't be doing at this point in its voyage. He rose from his bunk, dressed, slipped the Mark IV Hunter into a holster at the base of his spine, and went to find out what was happening. He took the elevator up to the bridge and was met by a very irate Captain Zhang Wei.

"What's going on?" Malik asked, as he glanced around at the activity on the bridge.

"Your passenger. She's taken the lifeboat. Gone. Escaped." Wei flapped a hand toward the stern of the ship, indicating where the lifeboat had been mounted.

"What? When?"

"Twenty minutes ago. She's also ditched our fast rescue craft. It's in the water." Wei swung his arm around gesturing toward the ship's starboard.

Malik couldn't believe what he was hearing. He had totally underestimated this woman. Never for one moment had he considered she would attempt something so... crazy reckless. He was no mariner, but even he knew that they were a very long way from land and she would never make it in that lifeboat, not even close. What was she thinking?

"We need to get after her. If we lose her there will be hell to pay." Malik poked a finger at the Captain.

"We can't. Our rescue boat is gone, adrift. We need to find that first."

"You're telling me we have no boats, no way to go after her?" Malik said, a hint of alarm in his voice.

"We have another boat, stored in the fo'c'sle. But it will take time to assemble and get it in the water. Then we go find the rescue boat. There's no panic, she's not going to get far. The lifeboat is very slow and has limited fuel, and it's a very long way back to the coast."

"We should go after her first, get her back now." Malik balked at the thought of wasting time searching for the rescue boat.

The Captain was not liking his authority being questioned. "You were supposed to be keeping an eye on her. Not let her do anything stupid. This was your job." It was the Captain's turn to poke a finger at Malik. "So now I clean up your mess. We find the rescue craft first. It has a GPS tracker so it won't take long.

It's also much faster. So it will be quicker in the long run." He turned to shout something in Mandarin at one of the crew.

Malik glanced around the bridge. He sensed confusion as the crew checked and double-checked the systems. "Why have we stopped?"

"You want to do something useful? Help bring up the other boat." The captain waved a dismissive hand at him. "Go, go."

Malik fumed as he left the bridge. There was still a considerable payday awaiting him when he delivered this woman to his handlers. But failure didn't simply mean he would be out of pocket. These were not the type of people you let down, they would demand reparations. There would be a contract out on him for sure. If he didn't get her back, then he would spend the rest of his life looking over his shoulder—for however long that might be. He grabbed a thick-padded jacket from one of the lockers and made his way toward the bow of the ship where the fo'c'sle was located.

It took them a good hour to bring the boat out of storage, assemble it, check the outboard and rigging, then launch it over the side. Fortunately, the lost rescue boat had a tracker that automatically activated when it hit the water, so they had a good idea where it was. Yet, it still took another hour and a half before Malik could see it being towed back.

Then they discovered that the fuel tank was completely trashed. Now it would need to be repaired. All this was eating up valuable time, making Malik ever more frustrated as the longer it went on, the further and further away Dawn Harrison would get.

By the time the rescue craft had been repaired, the new

morning's sun was beginning to brighten the sky to the east. At least visibility would be better. Malik had returned to his cabin to get into warmer clothes and check over his weapons, only to find they had launched the rescue boat without him when he returned. He was incandescent with rage, what the hell were these assholes playing at? Trying to make him look like a fool by putting her escape on his shoulders, then take all the praise for her recapture.

He spied the spare boat that had been pulled up out of the water and was now dangling alongside the deck. He made his way over to it and clambered aboard.

Captain Wei rushed over waving his arms excitedly in the air. "You can't take that."

"Why not?" Malik examined the release mechanism that would lower the boat back into the water.

"It's our only spare boat. We need it for emergencies," the Captain said, as if this should be obvious to anyone but an idiot.

"This is a goddamn emergency, you moron," Malik barked back.

"No, no, you stay, go back to your cabin, we clean up your mess." Captain Wei was becoming more agitated at this insubordination.

Malik restrained himself from climbing back out of the boat and punching Wei in the face. It was clear to him that this guy was trying to look like he was the hero of the day. But Malik was not taking any of that crap. He reached out and snatched a handheld radio from one of the crew, then pulled out his gun, and pointed it at the captain. "Get this boat in the water now or I will put a hole in that clean crisp white hat of yours."

The captain balked. He was not used to this level of threat. He flapped an arm at the two crew that were manning the ropes. They began to lower the boat down into the water while the captain poured forth a string of abuse at him.

# CHAPTER 33
# LONG SHOT

J eb Marlow sat in the main salon of the superyacht as it plowed its way through the gray waters of the Pacific Ocean. The space had been hastily converted into a temporary Operations Center with workstations and equipment duct-taped to every conceivable surface. At this speed, the boat bounced and slapped its way through the water, making walking, or even standing upright, difficult for those who didn't have their sea legs fully engaged. Several of the NSA team had already gotten sick—they had been banished to the outside deck to get some air and prevent the salon from becoming a stinking mess. Several others were clearly on the edge, looking decidedly green. But not so Agents Hegarty and Wiseman, and a small contingent of hardball operatives who were intensely focused on the various screens and readouts. The main monitor had been patched into a satellite feed and displayed a uniform gray expanse of ocean with a small orange dot at its center. That dot was the free-fall lifeboat from the Chinese container ship with only a single female occupant inside.

To some, like Hegarty and the state security apparatus, that occupant was Subject 19, the most valuable military asset on the planet, with the potential to start a world war. To others, like Neuromorph, she represented significant intellectual property that would make them rich beyond their wildest dreams. To Dr. Matsumoto, the potential to win a Nobel Prize. To Delman... well, it was hard to know what she represented to him now that he was becoming increasingly untethered from reality. Yet for Marlow, she was simply Dawn Harrison, the girl from the gym, the one he had had a crush on, the person he couldn't quite pick up the courage to ask out on a date. And here she was, cocooned inside an orange plastic tub bobbing along on a cold dark ocean with nothing but threat all around her.

A second monitor displayed a similar gray expanse of ocean, except this one tracked the container ship, which still hadn't moved. A third showed a graphical rendering of the locations of both the lifeboat and the container ship, along with the positions of Delman's yacht, the Coast Guard cutter, and a few other relevant ships on a stylized graphical display. Marlow could see that they were already far out to sea, making good progress. Yet still a long way from intercepting the lifeboat.

For a long time, they watched as the container ship launched a tiny vessel and set out to retrieve the rescue craft that Harrison had apparently ditched overboard. It was a process that took hours and seemed to make Hegarty ever more anxious. Several times, he could be heard talking with the captain of the yacht urging him to go faster, only to be told that they were at their limit, any more power to the engines and the ship was at risk of flipping. Marlow wasn't quite sure what that was, but he certainly didn't want to find out on a boat of this size. Another hour passed as they watched the two small craft being brought back onboard the containership.

"Why aren't they moving now that they have retrieved their boat?" Dexter asked, referring to the containership.

"No idea," Hegarty said. "But if they fix that rescue craft and launch it within the next hour, then we may have a problem."

A half hour passed with still nothing happening. Suddenly, all eyes turned back to the satellite feed as Hegarty's fears were realized. The containership had just spawned a small black dot that began charging across the water, a long white wake fanning out behind it.

"Crap," Hegarty said. "What's the ETA?" he asked a tech.

"Thirty-eight minutes."

"Damnit." Hegarty seemed to visibly deflate, then turned to Wiseman. "Game over?"

"Game over." Wiseman acknowledged.

Hegarty turned to another of the techs. "Inform the captain he can slow down and bring us into a holding pattern."

"What?" Dexter was on his feet, clutching onto a handhold for support. "You can't be serious, you're just... giving up?"

The NSA agent regarded him with a look of detachment. "It's over, we simply can't get there in time."

Marlow could feel the boat dramatically slowing down as

the vibration of the engines began to recede. "So you're just gonna let them have her?" he said, as he too got to his feet.

"No. We're not just gonna let them have her," Hegarty spat back at him.

"It's plan B," Wiseman said. "Only option now."

"And what, exactly is... plan B?" Dexter asked.

Hegarty gave him a hard look. "If we can't have her then neither can they."

"And what's that supposed to mean?" Marlow asked, hoping it was not what he thought it was.

Hegarty pursed his lips then cast a glance at Wisemann, as if seeking approval to explain. He took a deep breath. "We've just called in a strike on that lifeboat. We are going to eliminate the threat."

"What the..." Dexter's face went purple with rage. "May I remind you that Dawn Harrison is the intellectual property of Neuromorph and represents a significant dollar value to the corporation. You can't just... eliminate her."

"And may I remind you," Hegarty shot back, "she also represents a significant threat to national security. And so do you if you obstruct us in exercising our duty."

Dexter shook his head in disbelief, but he knew there was nothing he could do about it. He slumped back down in his seat, resigning himself to the inevitable. But Marlow was not going to simply roll over and let this happen. He thought about Dawn Harrison, the girl from the gym, all alone in that lifeboat thinking that they were coming to rescue her only to be screwed over, yet again. He had to do something, but what? Then it came to him. It was a long shot, but he owed it to her to try. He ran out of the salon and headed for Delman's suite.

He was met by Parker who had taken up residence outside Delman's door, ensuring that no one would disturb him. He pushed past her opening the door to the suite.

"Marlow, what the hell? You can't go in there," she called after him.

"Sorry, emergency." He entered, slamming the door shut in her face, then locking it from the inside.

Parker started banging and shouting, "Marlow, open this door. Open it now!"

He glanced around looking for something heavy to shove in front of the door but this being a boat, everything was bolted to the floor. He unlatched a bar stool from its cradle under the counter that ran alongside one side of the main room and wedged it under the door handle. It would buy him a bit more time.

"What is going on?"

Marlow spun around to see Delman standing in the doorway to the bedroom, stark naked, a curious look on his face.

"They're going to kill her," Marlow said. "Hegarty has called in a strike on the lifeboat, we can't get to her in time, so they're going to just... take her out," he spat out the basics as fast as he could.

"A strike?" Delman asked.

"Yes. I don't know all the details but we don't have much time. You have to warn her."

"We've slowed down." Delman was only now realizing that

the yacht was no longer powering through the water at top speed.

"Yes, yes, they've given up the rescue attempt, now they're going to blow her out of the water. But you can connect with your AI glasses, send her a message. You still have them, don't you?"

Delman glanced over at the bedside locker where the glasses still sat, exactly where Dexter had placed them. "Yes. But I don't do that anymore. I made a solemn vow never to use them again. I'm strictly organic now," Delman said.

"What? Are you crazy?"

"No. I've never been more sane. I never realized how much I was corrupted by technology. Now I'm at one with the real world, with the sea lions, and it's so much better."

"What?" Marlow couldn't believe what he was hearing. "But this is Dawn Harrison, the most important human on the planet, you said so yourself."

"That was a different me. The new me has realized that what I was trying to do back then was... well, suboptimal. If we want to save humanity, then it's time to get back to the garden. Anyway... it's probably for the best as the world is not ready for that much cognitive power."

"Marlow? What the hell are you playing at?" a male voice shouted out from the other side of the barricaded door. "Open this door now or we'll break it down."

Marlow feared that he only had minutes, and Delman had completely lost his mind. How was he going to get through to him?

He lunged at him, grabbed him by the hair, and dragged

him screaming over to a chair. He shoved him into it, held him down with one hand, and slapped him across the face.

"Listen, you crazy little shit. This is not about you, it's not about the goddamn fate of humanity, it's about Dawn Harrison, a person who's had nothing but people screwing her over for most of her life. You want real? You want... organic? You want to get back to the garden, then show some humanity. You don't see the... sea lions abandoning their pups if they're in danger? Goddammit, man, you created her, she's your... child."

Delman's eyes were wide, his mouth gaped open, and he slowly touched his reddened cheek where Marlow slapped him.

"Do the right thing," Marlow pleaded, as the banging on the door grew louder.

Delman gestured over at the AI glasses. "You're right. "She is my... child," he finally said.

Marlow rushed over, grabbed the glasses, and brought them back to Delman. He sat for a beat just looking at them. "Yes, I must say goodbye to her." He slipped the glasses on his face, his eyes glazed over, and his head went back.

"Harry, you need to warn her, not just say goodbye." But Delman was gone, lost in the AI.

The door bucked, and cracked. They were almost in. Marlow ran over and put his shoulder against it. It would buy them another minute or two, for all the good that would do. It was a long shot after all.

# CHAPTER 34
# ROLL THE DICE

The eastern sky grew brighter as the lifeboat chugged its way across the vast expanse of the Pacific Ocean. Inside, Dawn sat munching on a food ration, a dry cracker, one of the many items included in the lifeboat's inventory. As she sat and ate, she was mesmerized by the knowledge that percolated up in her mind as she cast her gaze around the boat's interior. She knew the location and purpose of every survival item stored in the lockers; the quantities of rations, the nutritional breakdowns, even the molecular structure of the core ingredients. She knew all the materials the boat was constructed from; their strengths and weaknesses, their core components, the fabrication methods used in their manufacture. There was nowhere she looked that did not result in a flood of data streaming into her conscious mind.

Her ability to access the bottomless pit of knowledge stored within the AI that had been implanted in her head seemed like second nature to her now. Her brain was forming its own connections, its own routes, its own pathways to access this knowledge. New synapses were forming, just like with learning any new skill. It was becoming muscle memory and she was becoming more adept at seamlessly accessing this knowledge. But it was more than just a bucket of random information, a collection of stored facts, a vast encyclopedia on tap. It was cognitive augmentation, an understanding of how these facts could be utilized, how she could do things that would otherwise be impossible for the average person.

She had no doubt that she could probably take on any chess grandmaster and beat them with relative ease. Yet, at the same time, would she really understand the game? Would she be nothing more than a Mechanical Turk? To be the greatest chess player and yet lack any depth of experience seemed... unfair— like a quiz show cheat with a hidden earpiece.

And what use was all this knowledge if it still could not give her the one thing she wanted most, to know who she was, to remember her past, to feel all the emotions of a lived experience. The AI, Morph, was suspiciously lacking in such personal information, and even if it did have a dossier on her background, how would she know if it were true?

She was fast becoming the most knowledgeable person on the planet, yet in many ways, she was still really a child, trying to figure out so many things that only a history of experience could give her. She was literally sailing in a vast gray ocean of uncertainty, alone and afraid, with no one to talk to except the voice in her head.

'Morph?'

'Yes, Dawn.'

'Is anything happening? Are they coming to rescue me? Can you reconnect with the Neuromorph AI and see what's going on?'

'Certainly, but you will need to make the connection.'

Dawn put away her half-finished food ration and picked up the small sat-phone and switched it on. The battery indicator blinked red, it was very low on power, so this might be her last contact. She had made the fatal mistake of not checking it when she shoved into her bag. Now her only link to the outside world was about to die. Nevertheless, she focused her mind, established the connection, and immediately felt her mind being transported along the data-stream seeking out the primary Neuromorph AI. When it came, it was like a door opening to a vast cavern fizzing with energy.

Morph transmitted another data-dump, giving location, speed, health, and a multitude of other details on her current status. But what Dawn really wanted was an update on what actions had been taken since her last update.

A fast response cutter had been dispatched from San Pedro —she knew its speed, its crew quotient, its weaponry. But she was startled to discover that Delman's own super-yacht, Saffron, had been commandeered by the NSA agents because of its speed, which she knew to be the second fastest ship of its class in the world, more than twice that of the so-called fast cutter. It was also managed by the Neuromorph AI, so she tracked it down and went in search of data.

It was almost two-hundred nautical miles off the California coast. Delman was onboard along with the NSA agent, Hegarty, and a complement of other agents and Neuromorph people.

But it had stopped, something was wrong. As she interrogated the data-stream Dawn felt a new connection trying to establish itself. It had an urgency so she bent her mind toward it.

'Hello?' she asked, tentatively.

'Oh my god.' It was not an AI voice. This had a human quality.

'This is Dawn Harrison. Who are you?'

'Oh my god,' the voice repeated. 'It's actually you.'

'Who is this?' she asked again.

'Harry Delman. I'm on my yacht, Saffron. But, eh... you probably know that already.'

'I know a lot of things, but what I don't know is when you guys are going to show up and get me out of this tub.'

'Are you, eh... communicating using... thought?' Delman asked.

'Yes. I'm... sensing you inside my head. And the words you are hearing are my thoughts.'

'My god, this is mind-blowing.'

'Well, I'm real happy for you, but what's going on? Why have you stopped?' she asked.

'Humanity is not ready for you. I know that now,' he stated.

Delman was not making any sense to her so rather than waste time trying to get answers from him she instead shifted her mind to interrogate the yacht's AI directly. She found the satellite feeds of her lifeboat and the containership. That's when she saw it. The rescue craft from the container ship that she had sabotaged earlier was now speeding her way. Twenty-three minutes to intercept.

A tidal wave of alarm rose up in Dawn's mind. What was she going to do? She couldn't out run it, that was impossible. No help was coming, at least not in time. *Weapons*, she thought. Yes, she would fight them off. There were some rocket flares in the survival pack. Maybe she could fashion a Molotov cocktail or two. A spear from the emergency oars.

'*You are my child,*' said Delman, cryptically. '*I connected to the AI one last time so that I could say goodbye.*'

'*What are you talking about? You're making no sense,*' said Dawn.

'*For too long I was corrupted, blinded by the technology,*' Delman continued. '*But now I see. You are not the way back to the garden. That's why you must be eliminated.*'

'*Eliminated! What the...*' Panic rose up inside her.

'*I must go, they're breaking the door down. Goodbye, and farewell.*'

'*Wait...*' But he was gone.

*Eliminated? What does that mean?* she wondered.

'*If I may,*' said Morph. '*I took the liberty of interrogating the NSA comms from Mr. Delman's yacht while you were conversing.*'

'*And?*'

'*And you're not going to like it. But a US air force jet has taken off from Edwards. They intend to target you with a missile strike before the Chinese boat can reach to you. It will be here in fourteen minutes.*'

Dawn felt as if she had suffered a sudden decompression. '*My god, I don't believe it. Why?*'

'*If we can't have you, then neither can they. That's their thinking. You're too much of a security threat,*' said Morph.

Dawn wiped a bead of sweat from her brow and then held

her head in her hands. She had just run out of road, nowhere to run, this was the end of the line.

Or was it? She sat up.

'You know what, Morph?'

'I don't. Please enlighten me'

'I'm done running,' she said, as she moved over to the helm. 'It looks like it's just you and me versus the world now, Morph.'

'I seriously hope you are not thinking what I know you're thinking?'

'Damn right. If those NSA dickheads are going to target this lifeboat with a missile then I'm just going to turn around and drive it right up the ass of those Chinese guys.'

'I would not advise this course of action.'

'Well, Morph. That's the difference between humans and AI. Sometimes we just say screw it and roll the dice. Trust me, it makes for a far more interesting life.'

# CHAPTER 35
# HEADING WEST

D awn jumped back into the coxswain seat, checked her compass bearing, and then swung the boat around a complete one hundred eighty degrees. She pushed the throttle forward as far as it would go, then tied a strap around the wheel to keep it steady on this new course.

'I have no desire to unduly alarm you, Dawn. But I estimate less than twelve minutes until the air force jet is within firing range. After that, it's twenty seconds to impact.'

'Appreciate your concern, Morph. But I'm not planning on dying just yet.'

'True, you do have approximately twelve minutes to live.'

She unpacked the immersion suit, a one-piece, zip-up garment made from thick neoprene. It would extend her survival time immersed in the frigid waters of the Pacific Ocean. She also grabbed the two rocket flares, the jackknife, and the sat-phone and shoved them inside the suit, zipped it up, and pulled the hood tight up over her head. She moved to the stern of the lifeboat, opened the rear hatch, and climbed out. The day was bright, the air fresh and salty.

'Okay, Morph. This is it. Time to check out. I hope the cold doesn't screw up this implant, or you might be the first of us to die.'

'I appreciate your concern for my continued existence.'

Dawn sat on the stern edge, turned around and slipped into the water, careful to keep her feet away from the churning of the boat's propeller. She felt a shiver as the cold shock instantly reacted with her skin, her blood vessels constricting as her body recalibrated its thermal management. After a moment, when her body had adjusted to the new environment, she took a breath and looked up to see the lifeboat moving further and further away from her.

'I fail to see the logic of this action,' Morph said. 'But had you remained on the lifeboat, then you would not have to experience a long slow death by hypothermia, which I estimate to begin its onset in three hours.'

Dawn ignored the AI. She was watching the lifeboat grow ever smaller as it made its way toward the horizon. She bobbed in the water for a time until something caught her eye further off toward the horizon, coming in fast. It was the Chinese rescue boat. It coasted to a halt by the lifeboat then came alongside, keeping pace.

She could just make out one of the crew clambering aboard the boat and working their way along to the stern hatch. Suddenly, there came the shattering screech of a low-flying jet. Dawn looked up to witness it flash past and as it did, she could see the slow arc of a missile contrail as it streaked through the air. She took a breath and dove underwater. Not easy as the immersion suit tried to keep her afloat. Yet she got herself under just as the missile struck.

The sky above her lit up in a blinding flash. A second or so later, the shockwave hit her as it passed through the water, knocking the breath out of her, sending her tumbling forward. Dawn kicked and flapped as she tried to right herself, but then she stopped and let the suit float her back to the surface. Her face broke free as she gasped for a breath. The air smelled of burning oil and plastic; she could hear the splash of debris raining down onto the water all around her. Where the lifeboat and the rescue boat had once been, all that remained was a patch of burning oil, thick black smoke billowing up into the sky.

'*Forgive me if this seems inappropriate, but it looks to be a successful strike,*' said Morph.

'*Yeah, they don't mess around, I'll give them that.*'

Dawn floated on her back for a moment as she unzipped the front of the immersion suit and withdrew the small sat-phone, wrapped tightly in a plastic zipped bag. She carefully extracted it and switched it on. A small battery icon flashed red a few times then disappeared.

'*Damnit, it's finally dead.*' She tried a few more times, switching it on and off, with no luck.

'*That's unfortunate,*' said Morph. '*It seems we must wait and try to survive until someone comes to investigate. There will be satellite observation in progress to establish the success of the strike.*'

'*Yeah, but that could be a very long time, if at all. And they may see a person bobbing around in the water and just... well, ignore it.*'

*'I'll admit it's a distinct possibility.'*

Dawn let the sat-phone fall from her hand and drift down into the depths. She was pretty well screwed now for sure. After a moment, she began to swim toward the site of the strike, hoping there might be something that she could use as a float, maybe enough to raise herself out of the water to help offset the hypothermia that would eventually come. As she got closer, she thought she heard the buzzing of an outboard motor. She stopped moving, straining her ears to listen.

*'What's that sound?'*

*'A two-stroke outboard marine engine. Approximately twenty-five horsepower,'* Morph answered.

The sound grew louder and through a break in the smoke that now covered the site, Dawn could see a small rigid inflatable boat coming into view. One person stood at the helm—it was Malik.

*'Crap, I thought he'd been vaporized in the missile strike.'*

*'Apparently not.'*

She lowered her head in the water as much as she could and began to back paddle. Malik slowed the boat, examining the scene, looking around at the burning oil slick. That's when he noticed her movement in the water. He turned the boat toward the bobbing figure and pushed the throttle. As he got closer, she could see his body language change when he began to suspect that the person floating in the water was none other than Dawn Harrison. The boat sped up. Dawn considered what she could do, isolated and exposed as she was in the water. There was no escape; he would be on top of her in seconds.

*'Your best course of action is to hide under the boat,'* Morph said.

'Great idea, as long as I don't have to breathe.' But then she understood. The hull curved out of the water on both sides. Theoretically, she could keep from being seen and still breathe. But that was the theory; how to do it without getting mowed down first was the tricky part. She took a deep breath and dove under the water as the boat passed overhead. It was moving fast. Was he trying to mow her down? Had he forgotten how valuable she was to his Chinese overlords?

'His anger and frustration are clouding his judgment,' Morph noted.

'No kidding,' Dawn replied, as she popped her head back out of the water to grab a breath. She could see Malik standing at the helm looking around, trying desperately to find her. He was shouting. "You can't hide, you bitch. I'm going to find you and make you pay." With that, he pulled a handgun out from his jacket.

'He really does sound pissed,' said Dawn, followed quickly by, 'Options, Morph. What are my options?'

'You could simply surrender. Logically, that would be your best chance of survival.'

'You really don't understand humans, do you, Morph? That's the last thing I would consider doing.'

'Why? It's a perfectly rational option. Why would you not consider it?'

'Because he wants to inflict as much pain on me as he can get away with before handing me over to be dissected on a Chinese operating table. And please don't give me any more of that "wait for a better opportunity" line, Morph.'

*'Very well, but I would be remiss in my duties if I didn't point out that all other options come with a very low survival rate.'*

*'Yeah, but mainly it's because I hate him with a vengeance. So it's me or him.'*

Before the AI had a chance to answer, Dawn already knew what she would do. She still had the rocket flares shoved inside the immersion suit, but to use one she would need to get as close as possible. She raised her hands in the water. "I surrender, just get me out of here," she shouted out.

The boat slowed a little; Malik had heard her plea and dropped his guard a little. He slowed the boat down, stopping within a few meters of her. He tried to keep the gun aimed in her direction, but it was difficult as the craft bobbed and rocked with the swell of the water. He lost his balance for a moment and Dawn took her chance. She whipped out a rocket flare, aimed at the bobbing Malik, and pulled the activation cord. An incandescent ball of burning potassium nitrate shot out of the nozzle straight at the target. But the boat rocked again, Malik shifted, and the flare only grazed his right shoulder, barely deflecting its onward trajectory. Malik reacted quickly, firing a few wild shots in Dawn's direction. She dove for cover, bullets zipping past her in the water.

*'Dammit, I missed.'*

*'Get under the boat, it's your only option,'* said Morph.

This time, Dawn took the AI's advice and tried to orient herself so she could rise out of the water near the stern, before Malik had a chance to get moving again. She came up just as Malik engaged the throttle and the propeller began churning water. Dawn reached and grabbed onto a rope that threaded along the side of the craft, and hung on as it spun around in the water.

The boat stopped again and she could feel it rock this way and that as Malik moved from side to side, looking for her. She would need to move now, before he twigged where she was hiding. She felt the craft tip forward as he moved back to the helm. Dawn grabbed onto the top edge of the wooden transom with one hand, and took out the last rocket flare with the other. The boat began to move forward again and she raised her head up to see Malik standing at the helm, looking over the water as he searched for her. She gently pulled herself out of the water, over the transom, and hunched down low against the stern. Then she took aim.

Malik must have sensed a shift in the small boat's angle in the water as her weight was now added to the stern. He flipped around, gun in hand, and fired just as she let off the flare. The bullet slapped into her upper right thigh, and she let out a scream of pain. Dawn looked back at Malik half expecting another bullet to come her way, but the flare had hit him full on the right shoulder. He screamed in pain, and the gun was nowhere to be seen. Yet he was not down, and the rage that burned in his eyes began propelling him forward. He lunged, falling on top of her, and grabbing her neck with both hands.

"You filthy bitch, I should have put you down first chance I had. Well, now it's time for you to die." His hands squeezed her throat.

Dawn kicked and punched as much as she could, but she was pinned down and he was just too strong and heavy. She tried punching him in the face, jabbing at his eyes, but he just shrugged it off and kept squeezing.

*'Twist your body left as hard as possible, he'll counter. Then jerk right. This will give you a chance to reach inside the immersion suit.'* Morph's advice came at her fast, almost in an instant. She twisted left, Malik used his superior strength to keep her pinned. She jerked right, his strength now added to hers and they rolled. Dawn reached into the suit, found the jackknife, and, in one fluid movement, pulled it out and drove it into his neck.

He let go of her, his hands now grabbing at his own neck. His eyes widened in shock as Dawn pushed him off her and began scrambling away, moving toward the helm. Blood oozed from his neck yet his rage still burned. He rose up on shaky feet, one hand holding his bloodied neck, the other reaching for one of the wooden oars stored along the side. But Dawn was quicker, she rushed to grab it, snatched it away from his weakening grip, and rammed the tip into his chest with all her might. He stumbled back, caught his foot on the transom, and tipped over into the water. Dawn grabbed the side of the helm, pulled herself up, and pushed the throttle to send the boat surging forward. After a few moments, when she reckoned that she was far enough away from the floundering Malik, she slowed the boat down, slumped back on the floor, and examined her leg.

The bullet had gone right through the side of her right thigh. Thankfully, it was far enough away from anything vital, but she was still losing a lot of blood, and in extreme pain. She searched around for a first-aid kit and found one in a locker under the helm. She began to patch herself up as best she could, tying a tight bandage around the wound to staunch the blood, and popping several painkillers. Eventually she pulled herself up on one good leg, started up the boat again, and headed back to the approximate location where Malik had fallen over. She found him floating face down in the water, the jackknife still protruding from his neck.

*'It would seem he has not survived,'* said Morph, a little dryly.

*'Good riddance to him.'*

She looked away from the dead Malik toward the pall of smoke that still lingered over the site of the missile strike, a scattering of debris floated all around. Finally, she cast her gaze across the vast expanse of the Pacific Ocean all around. Dawn was in no doubt that those who ordered this strike were also looking over the area. She cast her gaze skyward and waved toward the surveillance satellite she assumed was keeping watch overhead.

*'So what now, Morph? Will they send in another fighter jet to finish me off?'*

*'Unlikely. You are no longer a security threat now.'*

*'So they'll send a rescue ship then?'* she asked.

*'Yes. Probably Saffron, Harry Delman's yacht, as it's the closest and the fastest. However, I must advise that it will still take many hours for that to arrive and in the meantime, you are losing a concerning amount of blood from the bullet wound. Add to that your already weakened state from prolonged immersion in frigid waters.'*

Dawn knew all this, of course. But she liked talking it out with the AI, it slowed her mind down and gave her body time to catch up with her brain.

'*You mean, I may not survive that long?*' she said.

'*I'd estimate your chances are slim. You need urgent medical help.*'

'*Then there's only one other option.*' Dawn took to the helm again.

'*Agreed.*'

She looked over to the east, in the direction of Delman's super-yacht, almost two hundred nautical miles away. Then she turned the small boat west, pushed the throttle, and headed back toward the location of the Chinese container ship.

# CHAPTER 36
# CONTROL

Dawn knew where the ship should be, at least theoretically. By aggregating all the directional vectors she had taken since escaping, and by doing some complex mental trigonometry, she could, with reasonable accuracy, calculate the approximate coordinates of the container ship. But would it still be there when she arrived? Had the crew found a way to reboot their AI and get the ship moving? Dawn had only one shot at this and if it was gone, then she would in all probability die from her wounds, aided by dehydration and prolonged exposure to the cold ocean waters.

She could already feel herself getting weaker. She slumped over the helm, clinging on tight as the outboard propelled the craft through the water at a rapid twenty-two knots. It slapped and bounced across the surface as Dawn pushed it as hard as she could. The many hours it had taken her in the slow lifeboat to get this far were being reduced down to less than an hour's journey.

'*There it is,*' she said with relief as she spotted the ship on the horizon. '*It hasn't moved.*'

'*This is fortunate, Dawn. Your chances of survival have risen considerably. I would put them at fifty-fifty percent now,*' Morph said.

'*You do know how to cheer a person up, don't you.*'

'*Thank you, but I suspect you are just being facetious. While I'm merely stating a fact.*'

The AI had a point. Dawn could barely keep herself upright as she clung onto the helm. By the time she slowed it down and came alongside the ship, she was fighting to keep from collapsing. A hatch—used to bring harbor pilots onboard when coming into port—opened on the side of the container ship. Two crew could be seen just inside lowering a rope ladder. One started climbing down. Dawn brought the boat in as close as she could, then killed the engine, and slumped down onto the floor of the boat. A moment or two later she felt strong hands grab at her, lift her up, and carry her back up the rope ladder. More hands grabbed her at the top and they slid her onto the floor of the side hatch.

She could sense five people gathering around her, the Captain, a medic, and three crew. This constituted all that remained on the ship. They were confused, unsure of what this sudden return meant. The medic knelt down, gave her a cursory look over, then ordered the crew to take her to the med-bay immediately, just as she had hoped. As they carried her, she could hear, and understand, that they had been trying to get the ship moving again. One or two suspected her to be the cause and wanted to literally throw her overboard, but the captain warned that she was extremely important and needed to be kept alive.

Dawn, for the most part, just ignored them. Instead she focused her mind on connecting with the ship's AI.

*'You have returned,'* it said in a very matter-of-fact tone. *'I have been waiting patiently for your evaluation.'*

*'My analysis so far, you'll be pleased to know, is that you are performing well above optimal levels. However, there is one last task you must undertake.'*

*'Certainly, please inform me,'* it replied.

*'You need to restart the ship's engines and head for these coordinates,'* Dawn instructed. *'Then drop anchor and wait for twenty-four hours. After that you will have finished the evaluation.'*

*'Excellent, I will commence immediately.'*

She immediately felt the rumble building in the ship's structure as the engines began powering up. This elicited a very surprised reaction in the crew, with the captain rushing back to the bridge to find out what was happening to their erratic ship. Dawn then connected to the Inmarsat constellation and sent one last data-dump to the Neuromorph AI informing it on what her plan was.

By then, the captain had returned, telling the others that the ship was still under the complete control of the rogue AI and had now set off on a new course—and there was nothing he could do to stop it. They all looked at Dawn.

She opened her eyes and spoke in a low, weak voice.

"Listen carefully," she began, in perfectly accented Mandarin, in a regional dialect used by the ship's captain.

"I have taken control of this ship, and it is sailing back to US waters."

An anxious murmur rippled through the crew.

"Your job is to keep me alive. If you do then I will insist that you are all simply innocent merchant sailors, with no knowledge or understanding of who you were transporting, assuming me to be just some eccentric traveler who likes traversing the globe on container ships... it's not uncommon. You will be interrogated, of course, but ultimately released and free to return home."

A stunned silence permeated the med-bay as they all in their own way tried to process what was happening to them.

Finally, the captain spoke. "It seems we have no other option than to do as you say."

"What about the others?" she heard someone ask. "We can't just leave them."

"They are all dead," Dawn said in a whisper. She was fading, her eyes were losing focus, sounds were growing distant, her eyelids began to close, and she drifted into unconsciousness.

# CHAPTER 37
# DRIFT

The container ship, now under the control of the AI, powered its way East towards the port of Los Angeles — consuming vast quantities of fuel as it endeavored to squeeze every last knot of speed out of the groaning engines.

Weakened by loss of blood, sedated by morphine, and lulled by the unbroken rhythm of the ship's movement, Dawn drifted in and out of consciousness. At one point, around nine hours after she had been dragged back on board and patched up, she experienced a brief moment of agitated clarity. She glanced around the med-bay to find the medic slumped in a chair, engrossed in a book, and keeping watch over her.

"Wh... where... are we?" she whispered.

He looked up, surprised. Then put down his book and came over and gave her the standard concerned look practiced by all medical staff. He gently placed the back of his hand to her forehead.

"You need to rest. You've lost a lot of blood," he said in a low tone, barely above that of a whisper. He then proceeded to load up a syringe from a small glass vial.

"What's that?" Dawn asked, concerned.

"It's just morphine, for the pain, to help you rest."

"Where are we?" Dawn repeated.

The medic was silent for a beat, as he considered if he should indulge his patient with answers. He then looked up and glanced out one of the small windows in the med-bay as if seeking a reference point in the vast grey ocean beyond. "We're around two hundred nautical miles from port — another ten hours or so at our current speed. That's why you need to rest now, conserve your strength. "He jabbed her upper arm with the needle.

Dawn gripped his wrist with a free hand. "What's... happening?"

"Nothing. Nothing's happening, just rest. That's the best thing you can do for now."

Dawn let go of his arm, rested her head back down on the pillow, and closed her eyes. But she was still agitated and confused. 'Morph?' she asked in her mind. But there was no answer.

She fell back into a strange drug-induced delirium, sometimes aware of her surroundings, of other people entering the med-bay, of snippets of conversation. They were speaking Mandarin yet she could understand, or at least thought she did, so her AI in her head must still be functioning. In a heated conversation between the ship's captain and the medic, she learned that a US Coast Guard vessel was now shadowing the container ship along with a superyacht, presumably Delman's boat, Saffron. But the captain seemed desperate to regain control of his ship and was convinced that Dawn was actively controlling it with her mind. He ordered the medic to increase the dose of morphine in the erroneous belief that this would unlock control of the ship. The medic refused, reminding the captain of the dire consequences that they all would face if she were to overdose and die. The captain relented, and the container ship plowed on through the ocean for many more hours — that is, until the moment when all hell broke loose.

As soon as the ship crossed into US territorial waters it was boarded by several teams from the Coast Guard vessel; they were not going to wait until it came into port. One team burst into the med-bay, ordering the medic down onto the floor, hands behind his head. Dawn became aware of masked faces hovering over her, examining her, shining lights in her eyes. Then firm hands gripped her and transferred her to a gurney which was carried out of the med-bay onto the deck and attached to a dangling rope. She had a sense of spinning around in mid-air as the gurney was hauled up into a rescue helicopter hovering over the ship.

More faces greeted her as the chopper landed down in a military base.

"Miss Harrison, can you hear me?" said a black-suited figure.

"Uh," she groaned in reply.

"It's okay, you're safe now."

They wheeled her into an operating theater. More faces, more lights, more frenetic activity. She drifted back into oblivion again.

# CHAPTER 38

# EXPECTATIONS

D awn awoke to find herself in yet another hospital room; bright, white, and clinical. However, her brain no longer struggled under the weight of a drug-induced fog. She had an immediate sense of clarity as she felt the cool of the cotton sheets, the sound of the air conditioner, and the vague scent of lavender in the room.

'*Morph?*' she searched her mind for the AI's presence.

'*Hello, Dawn. I'm very glad you made it through.*'

She was relieved. The very thing she had wanted so desperately to be rid of was still there in her head. They had been through a lot together, her and the AI. And she had to admit, she would miss it if it were gone.

'*Glad you made it too,*' she said.

"Miss Harrison, you're awake."

She looked up to see a pleasant-faced doctor moving over to

her. Dawn tried to speak, but her voice was a hollow croak. "Where am I?" she asked.

"You're in a military hospital on the Vandenberg Air Force Base. Top floor. B wing," said the doctor as she began checking readouts on the monitor. "You lost a lot of blood, we had to give you a transfusion. And they had you drugged up to the eyeballs. But you were very lucky. That bullet just missed your femoral artery by a few millimeters."

Dawn reasoned that 'lucky' should really mean the bullet missed her completely, but she wasn't going to argue the point.

She now noticed that one wall of the room was all glass, through which she could see several figures milling about, some of whom she recognized. One she was sure was Dr. Natsumi Matsumoto. The same person from that first day she woke up in the Neuromorph research lab. Matsumoto was talking, or possibly arguing, with a man in a very dark suit. Along with what looked to be a very disheveled Harry Delman. At least she thought it was him.

*'Morph, can you identify those other people for me?'*

*'Certainly. The two men in black are NSA Agents Hegarty and Weismann. They were heading up the team that took over Neuromorph and coordinated the hunt for you, as well as investigating how the corporate data networks had been hacked.'*

*'The guys who ordered the missile strike on me?'* she asked.

*'The very same,'* Morph confirmed. *'The person to the left of Harry Delman is Gordon Dexter, CFO of Neuromorph, and the person hanging in the background is Jeb Marlow, Head of Security at Neuromorph, although his position is rather tenuous at the moment.'*

*'Oh, how so?'* asked Dawn.

'Agent Hegarty tried to poach him, but then he went and undermined Hegarty by forcing Delman to warn you about the attack. So, on the one hand, he should be persona non grata with all concerned. On the other hand, his actions ultimately helped lead to your safe return. So they don't quite know what to do with him.'

'Interesting,' Dawn mused. She thought she recognized him from somewhere, but couldn't quite place it. Yet his face did look familiar to her.

"Miss Harrison?" The doctor was leaning over her and waving a hand a few inches from her face. "Miss Harrison, can you hear me?"

Dawn looked up at her, slightly annoyed that she had been interrupted. "Yes, what?"

The doctor stood upright again. "I thought I'd lost you. You seemed to zone out there for a moment."

"I was just... thinking. Is that a problem?"

"No, of course not." She stepped back, not sounding convinced. "It's just..." she glanced over at the group behind the glass wall. "They're anxious to conduct a debrief as soon as I say you're up to it."

Dawn sighed, "The vultures are circling."

The doctor responded with an apologetic shrug of her shoulders. "I'm afraid so."

Dawn shifted in the bed, sitting up a little, only to be reminded that she still bore the scars from her ordeal. "Aghh..." A dull pain rippled up from her thigh.

The doctor put a gentle hand on her shoulder. "Just take it easy, you're still very weak." She then went about inspecting the many bandages that had been applied to various parts of

Dawn's bruised and battered body. Dawn refocused her attention on the group behind the glass and watched as the conversation clearly developed into an argument. Fingers were being pointed, voices raised.

*'Morph, do you know what they are saying?'*

*'Yes, they're arguing over your future.'*

*'Jeez, do I not get a say in that?'* she scowled.

*'Would you like to listen in?'* Morph offered.

*'Absolutely. How?'*

*'Mr. Delman is wearing a pair of augmented reality glasses with an embedded AI — a kind of early prototype of the one embedded in your own cranium,'* Morph explained. *'However, Mr. Delman's unit is rudimentary at best, with a glacially slow audible call-and-response interface. But, I can connect with it so you can see and hear exactly what he sees and hears.'*

With that, a vision began forming in her mind's eye, like a window into another world. She could now see Agent Hegarty's stern face as he explained how the NSA viewed Dawn Harrison. *'She's still a threat to national security.'*

*'Nonsense,'* replied Delman. His head then swiveled to look over at Dexter, making Dawn feel a little dizzy. The experience of seeing the world remotely was playing weird tricks on her own brain's ability to make sense of the movement. She brought a hand up to her head to steady herself.

"Are you okay?" the doctor asked.

"Yes, yes, fine." Dawn waved a hand.

The doctor furrowed her brow in a frown, then continued with her inspection.

'*This is not for you to decide, especially given your recent bout of irrational behavior,*' Hegarty jabbed a finger at Delman.

'*I assure you, Harry's over that now,*' said Dexter as he turned to look at his CEO. '*Aren't you, Harry?*'

'*Yes, perfectly stabilized now,*' Delman assured him. '*It was just... an emotional patch I was going through.*'

Hegarty turned to look at Jeb Marlow who sat, one cheek on the edge of a desk, reading from his phone. '*Thanks in no small part to your wildly unpredictable Head of Security.*'

Marlow looked up at the agent and gave him a wry smile.

'*Yes, well Jeb did help me, eh... gain some clarity,*' Delman admitted.

'*You can't have too much clarity, that's what I always say,*' Agent Weismann added.

'*If I may,*' Dr. Matsumoto interrupted. '*Miss Harrison needs to return to the research department at RainMan BioTech so we can begin the process of evaluating and recording her cognitive abilities. She is an enormously valuable scientific asset that needs to be analyzed in depth.*'

'*That didn't work out too well the last time,*' Agent Weismann said, without looking up from a fingernail he was inspecting.

'*This is not about you winning a Nobel Prize, Dr. Matsumoto,*' said Hegarty. '*This is about the security of this country. You all need to realize that Miss Harrison is a strategic asset, one that we need working for us.*'

'*So you just want to use her as a weapon, is that it?*' Delman asked.

'*Actually,*' Marlow interrupted them. '*She does have the legal right to have the procedure reversed.*' He held his phone screen up to show them a document he was reading. *'According to the contract she signed with Neuromorph.'*

*'Yes, well, she doesn't know that,'* said Dexter.

*'I do now.'* Dawn's voice echoed in Delman's AI glasses.

He whipped them off his face, looked at them as if they were possessed, and then looked through the window over at Dawn.

*'Delman, you're not going all weird on us again?'* Hegarty asked.

*'She's... in my head.'* His eyes were wide, his face a mask of shock.

*'Uh, oh,'* Weismann said, looking over at his partner, raising an eyebrow.

*'No, seriously,'* Delman pleaded. *'She's hacked into my AI glasses. I think she's heard everything we've been saying.'* He carefully placed the glasses back on his head.

All eyes turned to look over at Dawn. She raised a hand and waved back at them.

*'Maybe you guys should come in here and we can talk about what I want to do,'* Dawn said, placing heavy emphasis on the 'I'.

They filed in one-by-one, Agent Hegarty taking the lead.

"Hey, wait. I didn't say you could come in here yet." The doctor didn't like her authority being undermined like this. She hadn't given the go-ahead and no one should disturb her patient until she gave consent.

"It's okay," said Dawn. "I told them they could come in."

The doctor gave her a confused look.

"Trust me. It's a thing that I can do," Dawn tapped the side of her head with a finger.

"Which is why we need to talk," said Hegarty, not giving the bemused doctor a chance to argue. He moved closer to the bed. The others gathered around looking like a bunch of school kids who'd been caught doing something they shouldn't be doing.

"You showed some very impressive skills out there on the ocean," Hegarty continued, smiling broadly.

"Oh?" Dawn asked. "Does that include dodging the missile strike you had targeted on my lifeboat?"

"Eh, well... my apologies for that," he replied, shifting from one foot to the other. "But you must understand the difficult position you had placed us in."

"It wasn't our plan A," Weismann added, opening his hands in an apologetic gesture.

"You are an extremely valuable security asset to us," Hegarty's tone turned serious. "By the same token, you're an extremely dangerous one in the hands of our enemies."

"So what you're saying is... don't take it personally," Dawn looked up at him.

"The ordeal you went through was actually a good thing," Delman blurted out. "It leveled up your cognitive abilities at an extremely accelerated pace. It would have taken months, maybe years to get to where you are now."

"That's why we need to get you back to our research facility," Dr. Matsumoto added. "So we can evaluate your abilities, and check the status of the implant."

Dawn looked from one to the other in turn. "And what if I just want it out of my head?"

"Woah," Hegarty exclaimed, raising his palms. "Let's not be too hasty here."

"Of course you'll need time to think it over," said Dexter, his tone soft and placatory.

"Yes, yes. There's no rush," added Dr. Matsumoto.

*'Morph, what's the most expensive hotel in San Francisco with good security?'* Dawn asked in her mind.

*'That would be the Presidential Suite at the Grand St. Martin, which is actually used for hosting high-level government officials.'*

"You're right, there's no need to rush these decisions," said Dawn, smiling back up at the group. There was a noticeable relaxation in their body language. "I still need to rest and regain my strength."

"Absolutely," said Delman. "I can even suggest an excellent nutritional program for you. One that I've been using for many years."

"I think you should leave that to her medical team," said the doctor, raising a finger at Delman.

"But I don't want to stay here," Dawn continued. "Nor back at Neuromorph. But somewhere more... comfortable, with good security."

"I can assure you that security's very tight here. This is a military facility after all," said Hegarty.

"True," said Dawn. "But it lacks some creature comforts. I was thinking more like... the Presidential Suite at the Grand St. Martin."

"Ha," Dexter let out a laugh. "Wouldn't we all. But let's not get carried away."

Dawn looked over at Hegarty, who was not laughing. Instead, he gave her a long, considered look. "Would it help in coming to a decision... favorable to our national security?"

Dawn smiled, "It wouldn't do any harm."

They locked eyes for a moment. Then Hegarty turned to Weismann and communicated something in that invisible manner that only spooks can do. Weismann nodded, took out his phone to make a call, and left the room.

"You can't be serious?" Dr. Matsumoto looked aghast at Hegarty.

"I think Miss Harrison is learning the first rule in spy craft."

"What's that, extortion?" asked Dexter.

"No. Keep everyone guessing." He seemed genuinely impressed.

Dawn looked over at the glass wall, behind which Marlow had been standing, watching. He had chosen not to enter her room, rather to stay behind and observe. She saw Agent Weismann say something to him then move off. Marlow looked over at Dawn, catching her eye. He smiled and gave her the thumbs up. Dawn smiled back then settled her head into the pillow. "That will be all... for now. I'll let you know when I need something else."

The doctor began herding them all out, doing her best to stay professional while at the same time trying to conceal a grin of admiration that was threatening to break out across her face.

# EPILOGUE

Some memories of her past began resurfacing for Dawn. Mostly random flashes triggered by the oddest of things; a car horn reminding her of a childhood vacation, a poached egg on toast invoking a memory of breakfast with an ex-boyfriend. Yet, these snippets did not add up to a whole picture, not even close. But they did give her some hope that she could, given enough time, get some of her past back, maybe even enough to stitch together a connected timeline. Still, there was a part of her that wasn't sure she wanted to know the entire life story of the old Dawn Harrison, nor was she sure that she even needed to know.

Her leg was healing well, yet it would be quite some time before she would be fully fit. She was feeling stronger with each passing day. Helped in no small part by the luxury she now found herself living in, even if it was splendid isolation, with twenty-four-hour armed security occupying the entire top floor of the Grand St. Martin Hotel. Hegarty was taking no chances.

She had eventually conceded to Dr. Matsumoto's entreaties that her implant be checked out, explaining to Dawn that there were very sensible medical reasons why she should. She had been through a physically arduous ordeal and the last thing she needed now was to drop dead from a brain aneurysm because of an undetected issue with the implant.

Hegarty and Weismann kept the pressure on her to join the team, help fight the bad guys, as it were. Dawn tried to remain circumspect. But that couldn't continue forever, considering they did have some leverage over her. That being keeping her brother out of jail.

Jake Harrison had been arrested and was being investigated for his role in revealing state secrets. Although, Dawn wondered how much of this was a real threat to her brother and how much was just a bargaining chip for Hegarty. Jake, after all, was well connected and could easily beat that rap. Yet, there was a part of her that took some small pleasure in seeing Jake sweat just a little.

He had been contrite, apologizing profusely for his part in inadvertently getting her abducted. He'd been stupid and never would have done it had he known... yada, yada. Dawn let it go, and Hegarty made the charges disappear.

As she sat here now, in her palatial suite, looking out over the grand vista of the San Francisco bay, she began to accept that life would never be the same again and that her future was anything but certain. What she craved, more than anything, was some return to normality — whatever that was. Something that would ground her, something she could turn to that made sense in this strange world she now found herself living in. Even a simple conversation with someone that didn't have an agenda, that didn't want something from her, would be nice.

An image of Jeb Marlow suddenly popped into her head, and she realized he had been the only person in this entire affair that seemed to genuinely have her interests at heart. She should really give him a call to thank him, if nothing else. So she focused her mind, sought out the hotel's Wi-Fi network, and established a voice connection.

"Hello?" said the voice at the other end.

"Hi, Dawn Harrison here. I just wanted to thank you for saving my ass out there. Sorry it took me so long, but you know, it's been a bit crazy these last few weeks."

"Dawn Harrison," Marlow answered with surprise. "Oh, I'm not sure I helped that much. Seems to me you did a good job of saving your own ass."

"I heard you tied Delman to a chair and punched him in the face a few times."

"Ha," Marlow laughed. "No. It wasn't quite like that. I was just... trying to get through to him."

"Anyway, I just wanted to thank you for all you did, for putting your neck on the line for me," Dawn said. "I'm sure it cost you."

"Yeah, well, they still don't know what to do with me at Neuromorph," he admitted. "And Hegarty is still trying to get me to work for him. Which I find hard to believe after I tried to scupper their attempt to eliminate you with a missile strike."

"Well, I'm very glad you did. And for what it's worth, he's been desperately trying to recruit me too."

"That's not surprising, given your... superpowers. Have you decided what you're going to do?"

A window suddenly opened in Dawn's mind. A memory of training day in the gym at Neuromorph. A memory of Marlow biting off more than he could chew.

"Hello? Are you still there?" he asked.

"Uh, yes. Sorry, I just got a memory flash of you back in the gym, trying to bench two hundred pounds," she said. "I think I had to help lift it off you."

"Oh, please, don't remind me of that, it's so embarrassing. It was my first day back after many years of living off pizza and stale doughnuts, and, well... I thought I could still do it."

They were silent for a beat, before Marlow spoke again.

"Say, eh, would you like to meet up for... eh, lunch sometime... or maybe just a coffee?" he asked. "You know, when you feel up to it."

"Jeb Marlow, are you asking me out on a date?"

"Eh, well... yes, I suppose I am."

Dawn thought about this for a moment. A date? It sounded almost quaint. It was the type of thing that normal people did, and she would like nothing more in this world than to just be normal... for a while.

"You know what? I'd love to."

THE END

## ABOUT THE AUTHOR

Gerald M. Kilby grew up on a diet of Isaac Asimov, Arthur C. Clark, and Frank Herbert, which developed into a taste for Iain M. Banks and everything ever written by Neal Stephenson.

CHAIN REACTION is his first novel and is very much an old-school techno-thriller while his latest book series, MOON BASE DELTA, COLONY MARS and THE BELT, are all best sellers, topping Amazon charts for Hard Science Fiction and Space Exploration.

He lives in the city of Dublin, Ireland, in the same neighborhood as Bram Stoker and can be sometimes seen tapping away on a laptop in the local cafe with his dog Loki.

You can connect with G.M. Kilby at: www.geraldmkilby.com

youtube.com/@GeraldMKilbyAuthor
facebook.com/geraldmkilby

Printed in Great Britain
by Amazon